7 Sister Mysteries

The Secret in the Attic

Ellen Miles

SCHOLASTIC INC.

New York Toronto London Auckland Sydney
Mexico City New Delhi Hong Kong Buenos Aires

*I owe eternal gratitude to my editor and pal,
David Levithan, for starting it all off and for his
continued support.*

ISBN 0-439-23813-7

12 11 10 9 8 7 6 5 4 3 2 1   1 2 3 4 5 6/0

Printed in the U.S.A.   40

First Scholastic printing, September 2001

For Karl, the best boyfriend ever, with love and thanks.

I love mysteries! I love reading them, thinking about them, solving them. I love collecting clues, watching for suspects, and doing my best to avoid trouble. I love to match my wits against a really good mystery, using all my brainpower to figure out the answer.

I've read dozens of mysteries, from Nancy Drew to Sherlock Holmes, but the best mysteries are the real, live ones, the ones you find and solve yourself.

And this, dear reader, is the story of a real, live mystery that actually happened to me.

Chapter One

I never get to go first.

To look on the bright side, I never have to go last, either.

That's what being a middle child is all about. Especially in a family like mine, where being thirteen years old and in the middle means being surrounded by sisters on both sides.

Why don't I just get this over with right off the bat? The fact is, my family's big. Huge, actually. There are seven of us Parkers (nine, including my parents), and we're all girls. Yup, female all the way. Not a Y chromosome in the bunch, as my dad likes to say.

It doesn't seem to bother him, which answers one of the most common questions I get: "Did your folks keep having kids because your dad was trying for a boy?" Poppy insists he's perfectly content with all his girls, and I believe him.

As for the other common questions, like "How much do you spend on groceries?" and "Do you have to wear hand-me-downs?" and "Didn't your parents ever hear of population control?" I'll just answer them quickly: Lots, you bet, and like, duh, they're not stupid. My parents set out to have a big family. My mom came from one (she has three brothers and two sisters) and loved it, and Poppy was an only child and hated it. They knew from the start they'd have more than the average 2.47 children.

They also knew they'd move to Vermont (where my mom grew up) and buy a big old farmhouse to hold all us kids. Which they did. And that they'd name their kids after characters from Shakespeare's plays, since they met in a Shakespeare class in college. (I know. How romantic is that?) So we've got some, well, unusual names. From oldest to youngest we are: Miranda, Olivia, Katherine, Ophelia (that's me!), Juliet, Helena, and Viola. Quite a mouthful. People always make a big deal about our names. I don't care. My parents raised us to like our unusual names, to be proud of them. I guess that's why none of us really have nicknames. Anyway, I like being Ophelia. Maybe as a way to balance our wild names, our family has three pets with really basic names: Bob is our big, dopey dog; Charles and Jenny are our cats.

So. Back to my whining about never getting to go first. I was talking about a hallowed Parker dinnertime custom. My mom knows firsthand that in a big family it's easy for individual kids and their concerns to get lost in the chaos. She insists that we sit down to dinner together as often as possible, and that when we do, we go around the table and each kid gets as much time as she needs to tell something special about her day. You're not allowed to just say, "It was okay." I'm always amazed when I'm eating at a friend's house and they get away with two- or three-word answers like that. No, we're each expected to spend at least a few minutes reporting to the rest of the family about what's going on in our lives. While I can't say I'm always in the mood, overall it's not a bad custom.

But I never get to go first.

We go from oldest to youngest one night, and youngest to oldest the next, "to keep things fair," my mom says. Fair? Ha. Once my sisters Katherine and Juliet and I, who are all "middlests," protested. We said the middle kids ought to go first, at least once in a while. My parents agreed that was fair, and we tried it for a bit, but the truth was it was just too complicated to remember whose turn it was. So we gave it up.

It doesn't really matter, anyway. Everybody gets a chance, and everybody gets listened to equally. Well, unless there's something really delicious and distracting for dessert.

So. Probably the best way for you to get to know me and my family is for me to tell you about dinner the other night. There was nothing special about that dinner. In fact, it was a pretty normal Thursday night in the Parker family, on a crisp evening in late September.

Oh — there was one special thing about it. We were all there. That means, first of all, that my dad was home. That's rare. Poppy's an investigator for the FAA, the Federal Aviation Administration. Whenever there's a plane crash, he's incredibly busy for weeks, checking it out and working up reports.

It also means that my two oldest sisters were there. Neither of them lives at home anymore, but they stop in now and then, Miranda more often than Olivia.

My mom loves having everyone there. "Isn't this just so nice," she'll ask about twenty times during the meal, "to have everyone together?"

She's right. It's nice. But it can also make for a long meal, since everyone has to have their turn to talk. If you have somewhere to be, it can be a little nerve-racking. The other night I had no plans, so I just sat back and enjoyed the show.

It was a "youngest first" night, so Helena, who's nine, started things off. Viola's nine, too. They're identical twins. But since Helena was born eight minutes earlier she considers herself Viola's elder. Poor Viola. Helena and Viola both have wavy dark-blond hair and blue eyes. They can be hard for people to tell apart on sight, but their personalities are totally different. Helena's more outgoing, while Viola's pretty shy. Which is why Helena often jumps in first when it's youngest-to-oldest, even though Viola is technically the youngest.

"We worked on science projects today," Helena reported. "My group is doing an experiment about mold. It's really cool. We each sacrificed something from our lunches a week ago and we put all the food in a box in the corner of the room. You should see what's growing there!"

"Yuck." Poppy helped himself to another slice of meat loaf. "May I just interrupt to say, Ophelia, this meat loaf is spectacular."

"Thanks," I said. Praise from Poppy — or Mom — means a lot. It's true, I am a decent cook. I've had lots of practice. Mom works long hours (she's a police dispatcher), so we all pitch in. We hardly ever try to make anything fancy. I've made the same ten or twelve things about a hundred times, which means I've gotten pretty good at them.

"Now," said Poppy, turning back to Helena. "Does Mr. Lewis have any idea what you're up to?"

"Not yet," Helena confessed. "But I think he suspects. There's, like, this smell . . ."

"Okay!" Mom said brightly. "Moving on . . ." She hates when we talk about yucky things at the dinner table.

"I'm guessing you don't want to hear about my group's experiment," Viola said. "It's about saliva."

"You guessed right," Mom told her. "Anything else you'd like to discuss?"

"Hmm," Viola said. "Well, I did my book report today. And I think — I think it went pretty well. Mr. Lewis said I spoke right up." Viola has a very hard time with any assignment that requires talking in front of the class. Once she even started crying in the middle of a report on Alaska. But she's been working on overcoming her shyness.

"It helps when you love the book," said my mom. "And I know you loved *Watership Down*."

This brings up another thing about my family. As you might guess because of our names, we are a literary crew. We all read like crazy. Newspapers, books, cereal boxes, computer manuals, ancient Japanese poetry, dictionaries — anything we can get our hands on. We read aloud to one another in the evening sometimes, which I know sounds hopelessly old-fashioned. The thing is, it's a lot of fun. We've even read through some of the Shakespeare plays our namesakes appear in, each of us taking a part. *Hamlet*, the play Ophelia appears in, is not my favorite. I'd have to pick *Macbeth*.

Oh, here's something else you should know: Besides being a big reader, I also happen to just plain love words. Interesting words, long words, beautiful words, silly words. In fact, you could say I collect words. When I hear or read one I like, I write it down, find out what it means and how it's pronounced, and try to make it part of my life.

But I've always hated it when parents or teachers order you to "look it up" when you ask what a new word means. Why can't they just tell you? So, I'll give you a break. If I use an unusual word from my collection, say, *niveous*, I'll attach a number to it, and you'll find its meaning at the bottom of the page. Like this: "I adore the niveous[1] landscapes of January."

Anyway, back to Viola. Poppy asked her to give us a sample of what she'd said during her book report, and she told us a little about the book, which had to do with talking rabbits. Not my cup of tea, but hey, I'm glad she liked it.

Then it was Juliet's turn.

"Nothing happened today!" Juliet told us. "I swear. Nothing. I have nothing to report. Zip. Zilch. Zero." She crossed her arms, waiting to be challenged. Juliet is eleven. She has straight brown

---

[1]niveous: having to do with snow; snowy

hair and hazel eyes, and is very much her own person. Not shy. Not quiet. Juliet is straightforward and fiercely independent and pertinacious[2]. And loyal. She may not be the easiest of my sisters to get along with, but if anyone in the family needs defending, Juliet is the one to do it. Nobody can cross a Parker without hearing from Juliet.

Poppy and Mom exchanged a look. "Okay," Poppy said mildly. "That happens once in a while. We'll go right on to Ophelia."

Juliet looked surprised. Then, just for a second, disappointed. She set her jaw and nodded. "Fine," she said. "Good."

Poppy turned to me. "Ophelia? Tell us about your day. Was it a first-rate day?"

"And are you going to explain that disastrous bang trim?" Katherine asked. "Inquiring minds want to know."

I felt for my bangs. Katherine always knows how to get to me.

I'd cut them that afternoon. They were in my eyes and driving me crazy. Maybe I'd chopped off a little more than I'd meant to. And, okay, I looked a little geeky because of it. But did she have to point that out? I made a face at her.

[2]pertinacious: stubborn; can't let things go

She made a face back. Then she gave me this fake *I understand* smile. "That's okay," she said. "They'll grow back." I hate that patronizing[3] older-sister voice. I mean, she may be fourteen, but she's only eleven months older than me.

"Katherine," Poppy said, with that warning tone in his voice.

"Yes, Poppy?"

He glowered at her.

She dropped her eyes. "Sorry," she said, to nobody in particular.

"Go on, Ophelia," urged my mom. "Do you have news?"

I did. But was I ready to share it? I have this thing: I can be shy about talking about myself. I'd rather ask other people about *their* lives than talk about my own. Mom says that's what makes me special. She says I have a way of making people feel comfortable right away, so that they open up to me. I don't know. I think she's just trying to make me feel better. I don't feel special at all. I'm the middle child. I'm average looking, not totally gorgeous like Katherine. I'm smart, but not super-smart like Olivia. I can throw a ball, but I'm not a jock like Helena. I'm not *best* at anything. I'm just boring old me. Still, boring old me did have

[3]patronizing: putting down in a scornful way

some news for once, and I figured I might as well spill it.

"I do," I said. "Big news. There's going to be a new literary magazine at school."

"Wonderful," said Poppy. "Spectacular news."

"And I want to be editor," I added, almost in a whisper. I wasn't quite ready to go public with that information yet, but somehow it slipped out. I did want to be editor. I wanted it badly. More than I'd wanted anything in a long, long time.

Katherine let out a hoot. "You?" she asked.

"Why not?"

"Yes, Katherine, why not?" Poppy asked, raising his eyebrows.

Olivia spoke up. "I think Ophelia would make a great editor," she said.

I shot her a grateful look. Olivia and I have a special relationship. It's not exactly a secret that I'm her favorite little sister. She looks out for me, gives me her best hand-me-downs, and is always there for me to talk to.

"Sure she would," said Katherine. "But I'd make an even better one. And I want the job, too."

"Hmm . . ." Poppy waggled his eyebrows. "This could get interesting. It seems we've moved on to Katherine now. Is that all right, Ophelia? Were you done?"

"I guess." I took a bite of potato to hide the fact

that I was upset. Why does Katherine always have to do this? True, she could be a good editor. She loves to read and write as much as I do, though she's more into poetry while I love fiction and biographies best. But I know Katherine. I want to be editor for all the right reasons: to further a love of literature among my peers, to encourage those who have no other outlet for their creative impulses, etc., etc., etc., yada yada yada. Katherine, on the other hand, probably wants to be editor because . . . I thought for a second. Billy Smallwood! That was it. Billy is the best artist at our school. He was a sure thing for art director for the new magazine.

Billy Smallwood is very, very cute. And wildly popular.

While I was figuring all this out, Katherine was talking. "I know I can get the votes," she said, tossing back her hair. Katherine has great hair. Heavy, thick, dark blond, down to her shoulder blades. It's hair you can toss around or twist into a thick braid or pull into a ponytail. No matter what she does with it, it looks great.

As opposed to my hair, which is exactly the same color but curly and never does what I want it to do.

I can get the votes. Katherine's words echoed in my mind. She was right. She could get the votes. If there's one thing Katherine is good at, it's getting people to like her. She specializes in that.

She was still talking, but I wasn't listening. I was talking to myself instead. *Don't give up. Don't give in to her without a fight.* I decided, then and there, that I was not going to let Katherine steal that job away from me. I wanted it, I deserved it, and I was going to fight for it.

And let the best Parker win.

By the time I came to that decision, the focus had moved on to Olivia, who was telling us about some complicated darkroom technique she was learning. Olivia's nineteen, and she's studying photography. She lives on her own in Burlington, which is the nearest city, and goes to college and works as a waitress. I think her life is totally cool, and staying with her for a night is about my favorite thing to do. Olivia, by the way, has the exact same hair as I do, but she doesn't even try to tame it. She just lets it go wild, and on her it looks great. Someday maybe I'll be brave enough to try that.

I don't think my parents know what to make of Olivia. I mean, they raised us to be independent women, but Olivia took that idea and ran with it. She left home when she was seventeen, not because she and the rest of us didn't get along but because she was ready to be on her own.

She comes home fairly regularly, to do laundry

and visit and "get Parker-ized," as she puts it. An occasional dose of family bonding seems to be enough for Olivia.

Miranda, on the other hand, can't seem to stay away from home. She's twenty-one and has been out there in the world for a while now. She's a police officer (yes, she and my mom work together) who's always getting awards and commendations. Miranda's engaged to another cop on the force, Steve Dunsmore. They've been engaged for over a year and I guess they'll eventually get married. But for now, Miranda spends more time here than at her own apartment. She's always been really close to our parents and she loves being part of a big family.

"Any major arrests today?" Poppy asked her.

She ran a hand through her short dark hair. "Nope," she said, after thinking for a second. "I spent most of the day trying to track down a runaway, a sixteen-year-old girl from Underhill whose parents are frantic. Oh, and I helped to reunite a dog and its owner. That always feels good."

"What kind of dog?" Juliet asked.

"A husky mix," Miranda replied. "Really cute. But those huskies love to run away. I bet I'll be picking it up again someday."

By the time Miranda finished talking, we'd all

finished eating. It was Helena's turn to clear the table, and she hopped right up and got to work. We don't waste a lot of breath complaining about chores in this household; there's just too much to do. We keep charts and we stick to the jobs we're assigned, otherwise we'd all suffer.

Dessert was apple crumb pie from the East Hill Farm roadside stand. My favorite fall dessert, especially when there's vanilla ice cream to go with it. As we ate, Mom and Poppy took their turns telling news. Poppy mentioned that he'd just about finalized the reports on the last crash he'd investigated, a twin-engine plane that went down in New Hampshire. And then Mom told us about the new member of her Thursday-night recorder group.

I had no idea that this less-than-fascinating news flash was going to be the beginning of everything.

"He seems like a nice guy," my mom was saying as she scraped up the last bite of her dessert. "Michael, his name is. He and his family just moved up here. He plays alto recorder and he was so happy to find out about our group."

Mom plays recorder music with a small group of friends every Thursday night. She's been doing it for years. Once a year the group has a recital and we all go to it. They're not the Beatles (my favorite group these days), but they're okay.

"Kids?" Poppy asked.

"Just two."

I bet they both get plenty of time in the bathroom. That's what I automatically think when I hear about small families.

"How old?" Helena asked.

Mom thought for a second. "As a matter of fact, I think they're about your age. Maybe nine or ten. Any new kids in your class recently?"

"This girl, Gwen," Helena said. "She just started last week."

"Gwen. That sounds right. I bet that's her." My mom sneaked a spoon over into Viola's dish. Viola eats like a bird and never finishes anything. We count on her leftovers for seconds.

Then Mom looked at me. Without exactly *looking* at me, if you know what I mean. She glanced my way and then back at Viola's dish. "I, um, told Michael I might know a good sitter," she said. "They need help with the kids, especially now, while they're getting settled."

"Mom!"

"I didn't promise anything," she said quickly.

"Good." *Grrr.* I hate baby-sitting. But somehow, I'm always the one Mom recommends to people. Not Katherine. Me.

I shouldn't say I hate it. I don't. It's just that, with three younger sisters, I do enough child care in my regular life. I don't need to look after some-body else's kids, too.

Mom glanced at me again, compunctiously[4] this time. "I think they might be calling you in the next couple of days."

I plunked down my spoon. "So what am I sup-posed to say?"

"If you really don't want to do it, say no," Katherine told me, like it was that simple.

"Right." I've never been great at saying no when people ask me favors. She knows that. So does Mom.

"But I think you might want to say yes," my mom said. There was something in her voice that made me curious.

"Why?"

"Because the house they just moved into? It's the old Bascomb place."

[4]compunctiously: guiltily; apologetically

Chapter Two

Everybody gasped. Really, they did.

"The haunted house?" asked Olivia. "Cool."

Miranda shivered. "I still have nightmares about some of the stories people tell about that place. Like about the coffin in the turret? Ugh."

The old Bascomb place (that's what everybody always calls it) is this old mansion up on a hill on the way out of town. It's, like, the quintessential[5] haunted house. It has a turret and porches and second-floor balconies. It's huge. And pretty ramshackle. I don't think it's been painted in about twenty years. It's just this hulking gray building, sort of sagging at the corners. It's been empty for a while now, but for a long time before that only one person lived there. That would be the widow Bascomb, of course. I don't think I ever saw her; she kept to herself. There was not a huge difference in the way the house looked before or after she died. The lawn is never mowed, so the grass is about three feet high. The barn near the house is collaps-

[5]quintessential (I love this one!): Having quintessence. Quintessence, if you're wondering, means the purest or most perfect example of something.

ing. And the picket fence that goes around the property is missing a picket or two. Or three. Or a dozen.

You can understand why people think the place is haunted. It just *looks* haunted. It's easy to believe the stories. And there are plenty of them.

When I was in third grade, everybody was telling the story about how the widow Bascomb's hair turned white overnight from fright. Nobody knows exactly what she was supposed to have seen, but it had to have been terrifying. Jason Springer said she saw a bloody hand hovering in midair, but I think he just made that up.

In fourth grade, the big topic was the way the lights in the house were always going on and off at weird hours. Also, there was this story about how, supposedly, someone sobs and cries at exactly nine o'clock on a certain night each month, which was the day and time some Bascomb family member died a horrible death.

But the scariest story, for me, was the one about the coffin that Miranda mentioned. I've never felt quite the same about houses with turrets since fifth grade, when I heard that story. It's about a guy, some ancient Bascomb I guess, who loved his little tower so much that he insisted on being "buried" up there when he died. So they nailed his coffin to the floor and just left him up there. Ick. I imagine him all sort of mummified. Some people say they've heard a creaking sound — the sound of a coffin opening — on certain moonlit nights. Supposedly somebody walks around up in the attic with a lantern on some nights, too. People have heard footsteps and seen flickering lights. Is it the guy from the coffin? Nobody knows for sure.

"What coffin? Is it really haunted?" Viola asked. I could tell by the sound of her voice that she was genuinely scared. Viola scares easily.

"No, of course not." Poppy's voice was firm, a warning to the rest of us: *Don't scare Viola.*

"It's just stories," I said, smiling comfortingly at Viola. Great, chilling, scary stories. Which I adore.

"I'd sit for them," said Olivia. "I'd do it in a minute. I'd love to get inside that house."

"You don't baby-sit anymore," Juliet pointed out. "You're too old. And why would you want to go into that creepy old place, anyway?"

I knew exactly why. Because of the stories. Because even if it wasn't really haunted, that house had a history. People had been living there for years and years and years. People had been born there and probably died there. It was the kind of place that had secrets of its own. Mysteries.

There was no question about it. When the guy from Mom's recorder group called — if he called — I was going to say yes.

Chapter Three

He called! Or, rather, she did. His wife. Her name's Gretchen Frederick.

It was later that same night. I was in my room — the room I share with Juliet — practicing scales on my flute. Juliet was lying on her bed, reading *Swallows and Amazons*, this cool book about a bunch of British kids who hang out on their own and go sailing and have adventures. She was deeply into it, stroking Charles the cat, who lay on her stomach, as she turned the pages. My flute playing didn't bother her, even when I screeched the high notes. We all read like that, with total concentration. It can take forever to round us up for dinner, since we just don't hear our names being called if we're in the middle of a book.

I used to share a room with Katherine, but we fought so much (nothing physical, just lots of squabbling) that my parents finally split us up. Somehow she ended up with a room mostly to herself. She has to share it when Miranda or Olivia stays over, but the rest of the time it's all hers. I don't really mind. In fact, I think I'd get lonely having a room to myself. And maybe Katherine does, but she'd never show it. Meanwhile, Juliet and I get along fine most of the time.

I finished practicing (I'm committed to a half hour a day, otherwise Mom and Poppy won't pay for lessons) and started putting laundry away. "Hey, Juliet," I asked, "have you seen my purple sweatshirt?" I could have sworn it was on the pile the last time I looked, clean and folded and ready to snuggle into. I'd been planning to wear it to school the next day.

"Katherine borrowed it," she murmured, without even looking up from her book.

I should have known. I might as well give that sweatshirt to Katherine. She wears it more than I do.

I heard the phone ring, but I didn't run to answer it. It's never for me. Lately Helena and Katherine are the ones who get all the calls. Helena's always arranging rides to softball games and track meets, and Katherine — well, Katherine spends a lot of time chatting and giggling with various admirers.

"Ophelia! It's for you!" my mom called from the bottom of the stairs. Surprised, I bolted out of my room. She was holding her hand over the mouthpiece. "I think it's about that sitting job," she whispered. "Remember, you can say no if you really don't want to do it."

I said yes, of course. Ms. Frederick sounded nice, though a little stressed. She talked fast, barely stopping for breath. Flatlanders — people who've moved to hilly Vermont from places like New York or New Jersey — almost always sound that way. She told me they needed a sitter for Saturday night. If it worked out, they'd need somebody a few times a week for "the foreseeable future."

After I hung up, I headed into the bathroom (which was miraculously unoccupied; I grab opportunities when I get them) to check out this zit I could feel forming on my forehead. Of course, it totally showed, thanks to my new ridiculously short bangs. I snuck a dab of Katherine's Clearasil and applied it, hoping for the best.

"Help yourself," I heard, just as I put the tube away. Oops. Busted. Serves me right for not closing the door. There's no privacy in this house.

"Thanks. I did."

She shrugged. "You obviously need it more than I do right now."

"Those people called," I said, changing the subject. "The ones in the old Bascomb place. I'm going to sit for them the day after tomorrow."

"Better you than me," Katherine said airily. "I'm so glad Mom always picks on you for that kind of thing. Who wants to look after other people's brats?"

"It's not so bad. And it pays. Hey, do you have my purple sweatshirt?"

She rolled her eyes. "Why do you always blame me when something's missing?"

"Juliet told me you borrowed it."

She grinned. "Juliet was right. Consider it payback for the zit cream."

I started to protest, then stopped. It didn't really matter. The way we all swap clothes around, you can't get too attached to any one item. It would only make you nuts.

I glanced toward the study door. "Is Poppy online?" I asked.

"I think he just signed off."

The whole family shares a room we call the study, which is on the second floor (there are three in this house) between the bathroom and Mom and Poppy's room. It's a cozy room with a couple of funky old armchairs and a threadbare Oriental rug. It's full of books, including dictionaries and encyclopedias and atlases, and there's a big desk with a computer that we all use. We each have desks in our rooms, too, for doing homework. But if we want to look something up or check e-mail or do some Web surfing, we do it in the study.

I stuck my head around the door. Poppy was sitting at the desk, writing something in a little notebook. "Can I use the computer?" I asked.

"All yours." He stuck the notebook into his shirt pocket, stood up, and stretched. "Don't stay on for hours," he said. "You should be heading to bed soon."

"Just want to check my mail," I told him. My friends and I have been e-mailing a lot lately. We do instant messages, too, but I like e-mail better because I can save it. I'm also on a couple of mailing lists, one that sends a word of the day and one that's about dogs in the news.

I signed on. "You've got mail," said the guy in his annoying voice. There were three messages. One was from Zoe, a forward of some chain letter. I hate those! I wish she'd stop sending them, because I always feel guilty when I trash them. Not to mention a little nervous about what kind of bad luck I'll get. The second was the word of the day, which was *refulgence*, meaning "a radiant or resplendent quality or state; brilliance." Nice word, though it doesn't sound like what it means. It sounds — smelly. The third e-mail was from another friend, Emma. She wanted to know if I knew what the math homework was.

Zoe and Emma each think of me as their best friend. So does this girl Amanda, who moved to Connecticut last year when her parents got divorced. She and I e-mail all the time. It hasn't been an easy year for her. Sometimes it feels a little

overwhelming to have three people who cons.
me their best friend. Not that they fight over me
anything; it's just a lot to keep up with. Me, I dor
have a single best friend. It would be too hard to
pick just one.

I wrote Emma back, even though it was probably too late. If she hadn't done questions eleven
through twenty at the end of chapter seven by
now, she'd be up until midnight working them
out.

Then I wrote Zoe, telling her about my job at the
Bascomb house. She'd be excited for me, but I
knew she wouldn't be that interested in whether
or not the place is haunted. Zoe's pretty down-to-
earth and mostly concerned with how her passing
is coming along or whether she'll be starting in the
next game. Field hockey is her life lately.

I neglected to mention that I'd deleted the chain
letter.

I signed off, managed to brush my teeth in the
bathroom with only two sisters present (Helena
and Miranda; we easily coordinated our rinsing
and spitting), changed into my favorite old T-shirt,
and got into bed.

I tried to read, but my mind was wandering. I
couldn't stop thinking about the old Bascomb
place. Saturday seemed a long way off.

*   *   *

Not so long, as it turned out. Friday flew by and, practically before I knew it, I found myself on the old, sagging porch of the mansion on the hill. The floorboards creaked beneath my feet as I walked toward the door.

I felt a tiny shiver as I knocked on the door. I'd never been so close to the house before, even though I'd lived within walking distance all my life. Other kids dared one another to peek inside, but I'd never been one of the brave ones who ran up onto the porch and dashed back, screeching. It wasn't exactly that I was afraid of the house, although I'd always found the stories about it pretty scary. It was more that I had a certain respect for the place. The old mansion had an inviolate[6] dignity, even though it was falling apart. Somehow it didn't seem right to bother it.

Now, standing on the porch, I was feeling a little shaky. What if the Frederick family was like the Addams family? Was the house going to be full of cobwebs and dust and . . . coffins? Suddenly, I was glad it was still light out.

The door swung open. Ms. Frederick stood there, smiling. She was no Morticia. She was the opposite of Morticia. She was dressed in pastels, her hair was short and grayish-blond, and her face

[6]inviolate: intact; not damaged

was open and friendly. "Hey, you must be Ophelia," she said. "Come on in."

I stepped over the threshold. This was it! I was inside the old Bascomb place. I looked around warily.

Inside, the house was almost as shabby as the outside. The entrance hall where I stood had once been covered in elegant beige wallpaper; now it was peeling and smudged. The stairs directly in front of me were crooked and sagging, and the banister was leaning to the left. The wide floorboards were scuffed and worn.

But the sun shone in through the big windows and, while it was musty inside, I could also smell furniture polish and — was that popcorn? In any case, the house was definitely inhabited by living people.

"Have you been in this house before?" asked Ms. Frederick.

I shook my head. "Never."

"Well, ask Gwen and Toby to give you a tour, then. They'd love to show you around." She raised her voice. "Gwen! Toby! Your sitter's here. Come meet her."

While we waited, Ms. Frederick asked me a few questions about myself. You know, the standard what-grade-are-you-in, what's-your-favorite-subject stuff. And she explained that she'd be doing some errands and then meeting Mr. Frederick ("please, call us Michael and Gretchen") for dinner. They'd both be back around ten.

I answered questions and nodded and tried to seem mature and responsible and polite — all those things that parents like, especially when they're about to trust you with their kids.

Then Gwen and Toby showed up. Toby, who was carrying a bowl of popcorn (so I was right about the smell!) was ten, according to his mom. He was a skinny, serious kid with big tortoiseshell glasses and straight brown hair that flopped into his eyes.

"Toby's into popcorn lately," Ms. Frederick — I mean Gretchen — explained. "It's fine with me. Better that than nothing." She gestured toward the girl standing just behind Toby. "And this is Gwen."

Gwen was nine. She was one of those kids with an older face, though. I mean, she wasn't chubby and smiling and kidlike. Her eyes were dark and thoughtful, and she looked smart.

"Hi, I'm Ophelia," I said.

They both said hello, but the conversation stopped there. I didn't blame them for being shy. They were new in town, and everyone they met was a stranger to them.

Gretchen checked her watch. "Oops! I'm late.

Better get going," she said apologetically as she slung a pocketbook over her shoulder. "Have a great evening. Help yourself to anything in the kitchen. You can have microwave burritos for dinner. Emergency numbers are by the phone. Fire extinguisher is just behind the basement door. Anything else? I guess that's it." She answered herself with a little laugh. Then she kissed the kids, gave us a wave, and took off, running out to the big tan car parked in the driveway.

Toby sat down on the stairs to finish off his popcorn. Gwen plopped down next to him.

"So," I said brightly, "want to give me a tour of the house? Your mom said you'd show me around." I decided it would be tactful not to mention weeping ghosts or coffins or anything. After all, Gwen and Toby had to live in the house. No need to scare them with a bunch of old stories.

"Why would you care about this dumb old house?" Toby asked, frowning into his almost-empty popcorn bowl.

Gwen rolled her eyes. "Ignore him," she said. "I'll show you around. Want to see my room? You can meet my fish. His name's Kermit. He's blue."

"Did you bring him here from — where did you move from?" I asked, suddenly realizing I didn't know.

"Connecticut," she answered. "Yes, he came

with us. Daddy wasn't sure he'd make it, but he did."

"So did Sparky," Toby told me. "Our cat. But he doesn't like this house. He just hides in a corner behind the couch in the living room most of the time."

"He'll get used to it," I said. "Cats don't like change much."

"I know how he feels," Toby said, almost to himself. I was getting a definite feeling that he wasn't thrilled with the move his family had just made.

"One time Sparky got his ear chewed off in a fight," Gwen reported.

That started a whole conversation about cats and their behavior, and the ice was broken. Gwen was talkative, anyway. Toby didn't seem to have much to say.

After a while, Toby said he was going to his room to work on his computer. ("Play games, he means," Gwen said. "He spends all his time doing that.") Gwen showed me all over the house, from basement to — yikes! — the turret. The door to it was locked, so we didn't actually go up inside. Therefore, I can't report whether or not there's a coffin up there. Once I got over my jitters, I enjoyed the tour. The place was definitely old and needed a lot of work, which the Fredericks were planning to do — starting with a big renovation of the attic. The house had tons of interesting nooks and crannies, including a dumbwaiter to haul things up and down between floors, a secret passage between two rooms on the second floor, and a compartment beneath the stairs big enough for a bedroom. I envied all the space they had; both kids had enormous rooms to themselves. Overall, I have to say that the Bascomb mansion was a pretty cool place to live. But it did not seem haunted.

Was I disappointed? A little.

I got over that in a hurry later, after I'd put the kids to bed. I was down in the living room, reading one of Gretchen's fancy home-decorating magazines, when I heard footsteps upstairs. I looked around and saw Sparky lying under a chair, so it wasn't him. "Gwen?" I called softly. "Toby?" If one of them had woken up, maybe they needed a drink of water or something. I didn't hear an answer, so I headed upstairs to check on them.

Both of them were fast asleep in their beds. And I hadn't heard any more footsteps. How could that be? If Gwen or Toby had gotten up to get a drink or go to the bathroom, I'd have heard them returning to bed, too. But I hadn't. The footsteps had stopped as soon as I'd called out.

I'd probably imagined them.

That was it.

Definitely.

Then I heard something else. A sighing, sobbing sound. It was so faint that at first I thought it was the wind. Was Gwen crying? I tiptoed back to her room but it was totally quiet. So was Toby's. The sound didn't seem to be coming from their rooms, anyway. It came from the attic — or maybe the turret. Slowly, I looked down at my watch. It was just a few minutes after nine. Sweat broke out on my forehead. I shuddered — and ran back downstairs to the brightly lit living room. I spent the rest of a totally quiet evening reading and rereading the same paragraph in a magazine story about decorating with dried flowers.

I didn't hear any more noises for the rest of the night. But it wasn't exactly a restful evening. At one point, Sparky nearly gave me a heart attack when he jumped up, gave a loud meow, and galloped out of the room as if something was chasing him. Just a psycho-kitty moment, probably. Jenny and Charles do that sometimes. Anyway, I was very relieved to see Gretchen and Michael when they got home.

By the time I arrived back at my house, I'd convinced myself that the footsteps had never happened and that the Bascomb place was just a house like any other.

Chapter Four

"So? Did you see any ghosts?" Emma arched an eyebrow. "Any chain-dragging spirits? Moaning phantasms?" She gave a fake shiver. "Baby-sitting at a haunted house. It's so cliché[7], like the plot for a scary movie."

I waited patiently for her to finish teasing. "Actually, the house doesn't seem the least bit scary," I reported. "It's just an old house, like any other old house around here. Maybe it's a little more run-down, but that's it." I'd made a definite decision not to mention the footsteps or crying sounds to anyone. After all, they didn't exist, right? They were just a figment of my imagination.

It was Monday morning. We were sitting under our favorite maple tree in front of U-28. That's the name of our school. It's a big old red brick building with two newer wings. The *U* stands for Union, which means that kids from lots of different small-town elementary schools end up here for middle and high school. First bell was due to ring

[7]cliché: an overused idea or phrase

35

in a few minutes, but it was a sunny fall morning and I was in no hurry to go inside.

This was the first time I'd talked to Emma and Zoe since my sitting job. Poppy had kept me busy on Sunday, helping to rake leaves. I'd also gone with him to the recycling center to drop off a month's worth of bottles, cans, and newspapers. I hadn't had a chance to call anybody.

"Oh, well." Zoe shrugged. "No ghosts, no spirits. What were the kids like?"

"Okay. The boy is kind of quiet, which is nice. No running around with toy guns and yelling, like some boys. And the girl seems friendly."

"Cool," Emma said. "Are you going to sit for them again?"

I nodded. "Sure. I could use the money. And they really need the help. Both parents seem incredibly busy."

Zoe sighed. "Like, who isn't? I can't believe how much homework Mr. Fields is giving us in social studies. Plus I have track practice every day after school, and field hockey tournaments both days every weekend. I have a huge test coming up in Spanish. And on top of that, my mom expects me to take the dog to obedience classes."

"Obedience classes? What for?"

"He keeps jumping up on everybody and begging at the table. Mom says it's my responsibility because I was the one who wanted to get him." Zoe made a face. "I guess she's kind of right. Anyway, it might be fun. Want to bring Bob? We could go together!"

I had to laugh at the idea of Bob at obedience classes. He'd probably start out by licking the teacher to death. "No, thanks. I'm pretty busy, too. And I'm about to get busier."

My friends didn't know about the new literary magazine yet. I'd only found out about it because I'd stayed after class to talk to Ms. Cooper, my English teacher, about her herb garden. She wants to put one in, and I'd told her I'd help, since Poppy and I made one last year. She let it slip that she was going to be adviser for the magazine. I figured there'd be an official announcement about it during homeroom.

"Busier with what?" Emma asked, just as the first bell rang. "Oh, no! Tell me at lunch. If I'm late one more time I'll get detention." She jumped up and took off for the front door.

"Busier with what?" Zoe echoed.

"You'll find out," I told her, trying to sound mysterious. I got to my feet and grabbed my backpack. "Coming?" I asked.

"Not until you tell me," she said, staying put.

"No time!" I reached out a hand to help her up. We had about ten seconds to get to our lockers and then to homeroom.

We're in the same homeroom, which is very cool. Our teacher is Mr. Mires, which is even cooler. He's also our health teacher. He's actually funny, unlike those teachers who *think* they're funny. There are plenty of those around. It's so embarrassing when they crack lame jokes. You have to either pretend to laugh or sit there with a straight face and make them feel bad.

Everybody likes Mr. Mires. He tells us stories about what his kids did over the weekend, or jokes about stuff in the news. He's always entertaining.

"Good morning, people," he said as we all scrambled into our seats. "You all look ready for another wild and wacky week at U-28."

We groaned.

He was taking attendance as we sat there, making check marks on a form. "Anybody do anything fun over the weekend?" he asked.

Jason Springer raised his hand. "I went to a cool movie," he said. "Like, there was this dude who had, like, a thing implanted in his head, and these other dudes were trying to chase him down, like, on motorcycles and —"

I let my head fall to my desk. Jason is *so* boring. He's been boring since second grade.

Thankfully, Mr. Mires interrupted him. "Whoa! Don't give away the ending and ruin it for us," he told Jason.

"Oh, right." Jason pretended to zip his lip. "Anyway, check it out. It's called *Final Vengeance*."

"Thanks for the review, Mr. Springer. Anybody else?"

Alyssa Manley started to say something about her cousin's birthday party, but just then the loudspeaker started putting out its usual morning static. Mr. Mires held up a hand. "Hold that thought, Alyssa. Time for announcements."

After a few more crackles, a voice came over the loudspeaker. It was Ms. Davis, the assistant principal. She reads the announcements every morning, which is — well, it's a drag. She talks in a monotone that makes everything sound incredibly bland and boring. Not that most of it is all that exciting to start with, but still. Some people might put a little sparkle into it, you know? Not Ms. Davis.

"It's almost time for the Fall Frolic," she droned. "Get your tickets at lunchtime at the table outside the cafeteria."

If the sixth graders were depending on her for advertising, the Fall Frolic was going to be a huge flop this year. It's usually a lot of fun: There's a dance, plus a carnival with dunking booths and games. But you'd never know it from Ms. Davis's voice. She made it sound about as much fun as cleaning out the cat's litter box.

She made a couple of other announcements. A little knot was forming in my stomach as I waited for the important one to come along. Finally, she got to it.

"Ms. Cooper has asked me to announce that there will soon be a new literary magazine for U-28. It will have a student staff and will publish student work. Ms. Cooper will be adviser. The first planning meeting will be held this afternoon. Interested students should come to the computer lab just after the final bell."

It was stupid, but suddenly I felt hot all over. I could feel Zoe's eyes on my back. She was sitting behind me, and I knew *she* knew that this was what I'd been talking about earlier. I turned to look at her. She arched her eyebrows. I gave her the slightest nod. She arched her eyebrows even higher.

Ms. Davis droned on for a while longer. Then, finally, she finished announcements and the staticky loudspeaker shut off. Relief.

"Well," said Mr. Mires, stretching. "Lots going on. And the bell's about to ring, so I guess we'll have to hear from Alyssa tomorrow. Can you wait until then?"

40

She nodded.

The bell rang. "Off with you all, then." Mr. Mires made little shooing motions at us. "Enjoy your day!"

Zoe caught up with me as we left the room. "So?" she asked. "That was it? You're going to write for the new magazine? That's so cool!"

I shook my head. "I'm not going to write," I told her. "I mean, I might. But really" — I looked around to see if anyone was listening — "I want to be editor." I don't know why I felt shy about it, but I did.

"Whoa! Editor. Excellent. You'll be great! The best."

Zoe is always supportive. She probably had no idea what an editor does, exactly. But she knew I'd be great at it. "Thanks. But I don't have the job yet."

"You will."

"I'm not so sure. Guess who else wants it?"

Katherine picked that moment to stroll by, surrounded by a group of boys who followed her like — what are those birds that think you're their mother if you're there when they hatch? Geese? Anyway, they were all following her, ignoring everything else around them. I don't think they'd have noticed me if I was standing on my head singing "Happy Birthday" at the top of my lungs!

I watched her go by. She put no effort into keeping the boys' attention. All she had to do was smile at one, or lay a hand on another's shoulder for a second. She was probably reciting poetry in her mind at the same time. Katherine loves to memorize long poems.

I jutted my chin at her receding back. "That's who," I said.

"Katherine?" Zoe stared at me. "You're kidding! She wants the job?"

I nodded.

Zoe blinked. "Uh-oh."

"Oh, thanks a lot!" So much for my supportive friend. She didn't think I had a chance against Katherine.

"I mean, I didn't mean —"

"Never mind," I said. "You're right. It won't be easy. But I still think I can get the job. Anyway, I'm going to try."

"Cool." She patted my shoulder. "I'll help if I can."

The bell rang and we went our separate ways.

The day crept by. It was funny: I was looking forward to the meeting, but dreading it, too. Poppy's always telling me to try to "live in the moment," because I tend to be a worrier, but it's not so easy. Especially when the moment isn't too fascinating, like in social studies, where we're doing "How a Bill Becomes a Law."

Zoe and I had lunch together, but I wouldn't let her talk about the magazine. I didn't want to jinx the thing. Instead, I asked questions about her field hockey tournaments, even though I don't know a push pass from a corner.

Finally, the moment of truth arrived. Last bell. Time to get myself to the computer lab. Guess what happened? As soon as I walked in and saw Ms. Cooper's friendly face, my disquietude[8] dropped away. It was like I realized I belonged in that room, along with Bradley White and Matthew Kemp and Martha Baer and Sally Tompkins and all the other kids who like to read and write. Even Katherine. We all had something in common, and we were all totally psyched about the new magazine. There wasn't anything to be nervous about after all. I was glad, even if this new, calm feeling proved to be fugacious[9].

Ms. Cooper led the meeting. She's so cool. "What I want to do today is just talk a little about ideas," she said. "We won't decide anything. We'll just brainstorm. Over the next couple of weeks we'll need to think of a name for the magazine and get an idea of what it'll look like and how often we'd like to put it out. We need to talk about how

[8]disquietude: a state of worry or anxiety
[9]fugacious: lasting a short time

we'll handle submissions. And we need to start thinking about staff. We'll need an overall editor as well as some assistant editors. We'll need people who want to do design and pasteup, and people to proofread, too."

Everybody was nodding.

"There's a lot to decide, and I want you all to make the decisions. This is not *my* magazine. It's yours. I'm just going to be here to offer guidance and advice when you need it."

"Are we going to charge for the magazine?" asked Bradley.

"Good question," said Ms. Cooper. "Maybe we need to make a list of all the things we need to discuss."

"I can take notes," Martha volunteered. She pulled a notebook out of her pack and started to write.

"I think it should be free," Katherine said flatly. "Why charge? What would we do with the money?"

"We may need it for production," I said, glancing at Ms. Cooper. Hoping she'd notice my responsible thinking. "Will we? Is there money for this?"

She nodded. "There's a small budget. But it won't last forever. We may have to think of some ways to raise revenue. Charging for the magazine is an option, but it would certainly be preferable to be able to give it away."

Katherine looked smug.

"Who's going to be editor?"

That was Sally. The room fell silent for a second after she blurted out the big question on everybody's mind.

Then Matthew spoke up. "I think Katherine would be great." He spoke quickly, and his face turned bright red. Matt is known for his dark, spooky science fiction stories. And for his not-too-secret crush on my sister. Apparently Katherine had already been campaigning with her loyal subjects.

"Anybody in this room would be great," Ms. Cooper said. "Why don't we hold off on that decision until we've talked over some other issues? I don't want the editor to be the supreme commander here. I want us to make decisions together. After we've established what the magazine will be like, we can decide who's best suited to bring that vision to life."

We all nodded. It sounded sensible. It also sounded nerve-racking. How long would I have to wait before I knew if I'd get the job? I looked over at Katherine. She didn't seem stressed at all. She assumed the job would come to her if she wanted it. I tried to calm myself and take the same attitude. All I could do was put all my energy into the magazine — and do my best to keep Katherine's assumption from coming true. I wanted the job more than ever, and I wasn't about to let it fall into her lap.

Chapter Five

Oh, by the way?

Nobody — not one person — has mentioned my bangs since I cut them.

The question is: Why not? Was it A) because they looked so horrible nobody wanted to bring up the subject? Or B) because they didn't really look so different after all?

Needless to say, I was hoping for B. But, thanks to Katherine, I suspected that it was A.

Chapter Six

"Hi! Oh, boy, we're crazy here today." Gretchen Frederick waved me in. She was holding the phone between her shoulder and ear as she answered the door. "No, no, I was talking to the baby-sitter," she told the person on the phone.

It was Tuesday, right after school. When I got to the Bascomb place I saw two pickup trucks in the yard. One was old and beat-up (dark blue with rust spots) and the other was shiny and new (red, with a sign on the door that read SUSAN DUFF DESIGNS). Now I had a moment to match the trucks with the strangers in the kitchen. There were three carpenter types in faded, paint-spattered jeans and work shirts. Two were guys, both with beards and mustaches, and one was a woman with a long braid of copper-colored hair. The fourth person, who I immediately suspected was Susan Duff, was a tall, thin, black-haired woman dressed in a cream-colored jacket with matching skirt and shoes. She looked classy. She had to be the one with the shiny new pickup.

"Look, I'm telling you I don't have any idea about the specifics of the will. If you want to have your lawyer contact our lawyer, that's fine. But we're not ready for company at this point, so a visit right now is impossible." Gretchen was still on the phone. She rolled her eyes.

I just stood there, fingering my bangs and feeling out of place. Gwen and Toby were nowhere in sight.

Finally, Gretchen hung up. "Sorry," she said.

I wasn't sure if she was apologizing to me or to the other people. "It's okay," I said, at the same time as the woman in the suit.

Gretchen rolled her eyes. "Everything seems to happen at once," she said. "And I've got an appointment, so I really have to run. Ophelia, this is Susan Duff, the architect in charge of our renovation."

Yes! I'd called that one. I smiled at Susan and she smiled back.

"Susan will be staying for a while this afternoon to take some measurements. And this is Lori, and Steve, and Mitchell," she went on. We all nodded at one another. "They'll be doing most of the work. It's good for you all to meet, since you'll probably be running into one another often over the next few weeks." She paused for breath. "So, let's see. Did we cover everything?" This was directed at Susan.

"Well, we still have to decide about that corner

room," Susan said, looking down at some blueprints that were spread on the table. "And the skylight."

"Right, right." Gretchen nodded. "Okay. I don't have time now, but we'll talk about it tomorrow." She grabbed her pocketbook, sunglasses, and keys from the counter.

"Fine," said Susan. "No rush."

Gretchen turned to me. "Ophelia, I want to ask you a favor. If the phone rings, just let the machine get it. Don't answer it yourself. If it's me or Michael, we'll talk to the machine until you hear us and pick up."

"Okay." It wasn't like I was expecting any calls.

"I guess that's it, then," she said, looking around the kitchen. "See you all tomorrow." She went out into the hall and called to Gwen and Toby. "Kids, Ophelia's here. I'm leaving now!"

"Bye!" the kids called back from upstairs.

"I guess I'll go check on Gwen and Toby," I said, feeling a little awkward around the adults in the kitchen. I waved a hand vaguely toward the upstairs. "So. See you later, I guess."

As I was leaving, I glanced at the blueprints on the table. They sure were interesting. Being an architect seemed like a cool job. My curiosity beat out my shyness. I turned to Susan. "Do you think you could show us what you're doing up there?" I asked. "If Gwen and Toby want to, I mean."

Susan looked a little surprised. Then she smiled. "Sure. I'd be glad to."

Gwen wanted to. Toby didn't.

"No thanks," Toby said flatly, when I checked in with him. "Not interested." He was sitting at his computer, which was set up near a window in his room. Lucky kid, to have his own computer! He was having a hard time taking his eyes off the screen long enough to answer me. At least the game he was playing didn't look like one of those gory, violent boy games. It had wizards and dragons and things, but no blood or exploding cars. I reminded myself to check with Gretchen about whether she and Toby's dad put any limits on his computer time. I figured she would have told me if they did, but it didn't hurt to make sure.

Gwen was excited about the renovations. "I can't wait until it's all done," she said when I found her reading in her room. "It's going to be so cool. We're going to have a room just for art projects, and Mom and Dad promised Toby he could have a telescope up there, in the library room. They think that'll help him like the house better. And Mom said I can take over the whole attic for sleepovers."

"A whole room for art? Cool!" I said.

She nodded. "I know. I like to draw and paint and make things out of clay. I even like to sew things, like rag dolls and doll clothes."

Sewing! "I have six sisters, and not one of us knows how to sew." I was impressed.

"Mom's an artist, too," Gwen told me. "She did that painting." She pointed to one of the pictures on her wall. It was beautiful! A blue vase full of white flowers stood out against a background of rich, deep colors.

"Really?" I got up to look at the drawing. I wish I could draw like that, but about all I'm capable of is stick figures and doodles like stars and moons. Oh, and I can draw a sitting cat. Emma showed me how one day during study hall.

"She's going to set up her easel in the art room," Gwen told me. "And we're going to have —"

Just then, the phone rang.

"I'll get it!" Gwen swung her legs off the bed.

"No!" I jumped up. "I mean, your mom wanted me to let the machine get it. We can go downstairs and pick up if it's your mom or dad."

I followed the sound of Ms. Frederick's outgoing message and found the answering machine in the downstairs hall. We arrived just in time to hear a beep and a male voice. "This is Graham Bascomb again," said the voice. "I don't mean to bother you, but I've talked to my lawyer and he says I have a right to inspect property that I believe belongs to me. I'll call you again soon to set up a time for me to visit."

The machine beeped again as the caller hung up.

What was that all about? The man sounded pretty irate[10]. "Bascomb?" I asked. "That's the name of the people who used to own this house."

"I know," Gwen said. "It used to be my mom's name, too, before she married my dad. That guy is related to her somehow." She gestured toward the machine. "He keeps bugging us. He says this house should have been left to him. He's trying to get it away from us!"

Wow. This was big news. The Fredericks were actually Bascomb relatives! Interesting. And there was another relative who wanted the house, too. It was like one of those family feuds over a will, the kind you see on soap operas. "Trying to get it away from you?" I asked. "Like, how?"

"I don't know." Gwen shrugged. "But Mom and Dad don't want us to talk to him."

Now I understood why Gretchen hadn't wanted me to answer the phone. This whole business

---

[10]irate: angry, upset

sounded complicated. The man didn't seem nasty or anything, but if there were lawyers involved it probably made sense for me to steer clear of talking to him.

"Everything okay?" That was Susan Duff. She came out of the kitchen, a rolled-up blueprint under her arm.

"Sure, I guess so," I told her. I wanted to know more about this Graham Bascomb character, but it didn't seem right to ask Gwen.

"Do you still want to see what we're planning to do upstairs?" Susan asked. "I'm just headed up to check some things out."

I looked at Gwen. "Definitely!" she said. "Are we still going to have a window seat in the library room? I think that's so cool. I'm going to keep some of my books up there."

Susan smiled. "I love window seats, too. There are actually going to be two of them, one for you and one for your brother."

"Ha." Gwen made a face. "He won't sit there unless he can plug in his computer."

"Maybe he'll have a laptop one of these days," Susan said. "And there'll be plenty of outlets. Anyway, come on up."

She led us up to the attic. I was glad to be with her and Gwen; after the noises I'd heard the other night I probably wouldn't have gone there alone, even in broad daylight.

"Wow," Susan said when we opened the door at the top of the stairs. She was standing stock-still in the middle of the big, open room, looking around.

"Oh, no!" I said when I took a look. The place was a total mess. Lumber and tools were thrown all over the place, like a tornado had been through the room. Nails and screws were jumbled all over the floor, and a can of yellow paint was spilled in one corner.

"Look!" gasped Gwen. She pointed to the far wall. There, written in dripping yellow letters almost a foot high, was the message, GO AWAY NOW!

"Who would do this?" Susan asked. "Who?"

I didn't have a clue. I just felt awful for her and for the Fredericks.

Susan led us over to a small table set up in the corner. There were more blueprints lying on it. "Oh, no!" she said as soon as she got close. "What a mess."

"What's the matter?" I asked.

She shook her head and waved a hand at the table. "There's paint all over these. I'm going to have to do them over." She sighed. "If somebody thinks this is funny, they're wrong."

"It wasn't me!" Gwen said. "I haven't even been up here. Neither has Toby."

"I didn't mean to accuse you," Susan told her. "I know it's not you or your brother. And I don't think my crew is responsible, either. They're all really trustworthy. I've worked with them before. And why would they make such a mess? They're the ones who are going to have to clean it up. But this isn't the only thing that has happened. Things keep disappearing from this room. The other day it was my favorite pen. And a notebook. The one I keep important lists in."

"But who would take stuff like that?" I asked.

She shrugged. "Mitchell says it's the ghost. He's such a hoot. He even claimed to hear a door slam one day, and he says he feels like he's being watched sometimes. He mentioned ghostly footsteps, too."

I felt a chill when Susan mentioned footsteps.

"Ghost?" Gwen looked scared. "There's a ghost in this house?"

"Of course not," Susan said, reaching out to touch Gwen's shoulder reassuringly. "There's no such thing as ghosts. Still, I can't help wondering sometimes."

I wondered, too. Mitchell was probably from around here, so he'd heard the stories about the old Bascomb place. Maybe he didn't believe in ghosts, either; maybe it was all just a joke to him. But suddenly, I was feeling a delicious tingle shoot up my back. This baby-sitting job was suddenly getting a little more interesting — and a lot scarier.

Distant relatives who wanted to argue over wills.

Slamming doors. Disappearing pens. Mysterious spills and nasty messages.

And maybe those footsteps weren't in my imagination after all.

Something was definitely happening at the old Bascomb place.

Chapter Seven

When I got home, Miranda's car was in the driveway. She was in the kitchen talking to Katherine. "Hey," she said. "Just in time. We're going over to Helena's softball game. Steve got roped into umpiring, so I said I'd come watch. Want to come?"

"Are you leaving right now?" I asked, opening the refrigerator door. "What about dinner?"

"There's some leftover lasagna. We can nuke that when we get back. I'll throw a salad together, too."

I thought for a second. Did I really want to go anywhere with Katherine? I wasn't exactly in the mood to be chummy with her. Then I thought about how happy it makes Helena when any of us shows up for her games. Her special fall softball league is almost finished with its season, so there wouldn't be many more games to see. I didn't have any other big plans for the evening; why not just go? Besides, I wanted to talk to somebody about what was going on at the Bascomb place, and Miranda would be a good listener. I grabbed some baby carrots for a snack.

"Okay. Did anybody walk Bob? Or should we take him with us?"

Katherine groaned. "No way are we taking him. All he does is bark at every pitch and try to fetch foul balls. He's a pest."

"I let him out for a while when I first got here," Miranda said. "He read his p-mail and answered it. He's fine for now." (Reading p-mail is our family term for when Bob sniffs at certain bushes and trees. You can guess what answering it means.)

I ducked into Katherine's room and grabbed my purple sweatshirt. Then the three of us started off down the street. Helena's game was at the elementary school, which is walking distance from our house. Cloverdale is a pretty small town. It's laid out around a big green, sort of a town lawn with trees and a gazebo where there used to be band concerts when I was little. We live on the west side of the green, on Spring Street. A big road, Route 20, runs up the north side. That's the road you take to get to Burlington. Across the green, on the east side, there's a row of stores: a health-food store, a general store, and an antique shop called Granny's Attic. There's a white church with a tall steeple on the south side of the green. It's all so picturesque. These days busloads of tourists who come to see the fall colors — we call them leaf-peepers — are driving all through the state. The buses love to stop in Cloverdale so people can take pictures of the white church surrounded by golden and flame-red maples.

Mom and Poppy are always telling us how lucky we are to live in Vermont. "It's a special place," Mom will say. "It's safe here, and beautiful, and unspoiled."

I'm sure they're right. Even though I've never lived anywhere else, I've visited other places. My class went to Boston last year for a field trip, and I've been to New Jersey to visit my grandparents. I like seeing other parts of the country, but I have to say I'm always glad to come home to the hinterland[11]. Some people might think it's boring here, but so far I don't feel that way. I might when I'm older, but right now I like it just fine. I like being able to walk to school or to the store. I like that I can ride my bike for a mile and be in the middle of nowhere, with cows in the fields and wildflowers lining the sides of the road. And I like not having to worry about crime. We never lock our door at home; we kids don't even have a key for the front door!

Miranda and Katherine and I walked across the green, cut through the church's property, and took a path through the field behind it. We crossed a lit-

[11]hinterland: a region remote from cities

tle stream on a wooden footbridge and headed up the hill, past an old apple orchard, to the school.

I took that route every day from kindergarten to fifth grade. I could do it with my eyes closed. I know every landmark, every stump and boulder in the field. I'll never forget the time Katherine "kidnapped" my favorite Beanie Baby (a bear I called Blackie) and threw him in the stream, or the time Billy Smallwood (yes, the cute guy) fell out of the big maple tree in the middle of the meadow and broke his arm.

Katherine and I were there when it happened, and we were both terrified. He fell from so high up! We ran over to him, positive he was going to be dead. Instead, he was laughing this strange laugh as he held up his arm, which stuck out at the weirdest angle. I can still picture it perfectly. It was a sunny day, with puffy white clouds in the sky. I was in second grade, and Katherine and Billy were in third.

I turned to Katherine. I wanted to ask if she remembered. But when I saw her face, I turned away again. I was still mad at her. We hadn't talked at all about the literary magazine. She had to know I was angry about her trying to become editor.

We arrived at the dusty little ball field behind the school just as Helena came up to bat. Her team, the Cardinals, was already ahead, four to one.

"Go, Helena!" I called as the three of us found a grassy spot for ourselves along the third-base line.

She looked up at me and grinned. The blue batting helmet she wore was a little too big for her. She looked really cute in her red Cardinals shirt, her hair pulled back in a ponytail. She kicked at the dirt, took a few practice swings, and got ready for the pitch.

Crack! Helena connected and the ball flew into the outfield. We all cheered.

Once the dust had settled, Helena waved to us from third base. If it were me, I'd be embarrassed by all the attention. But Helena loves it. Her teammates were going wild, too.

Helena's friend Megan came up next and walked after four totally wild pitches. Then Jenna Smallwood (yep, Billy's little sister) hit a home run, which brought in three runs. Helena's teammates lined up near the plate to high-five the three of them as they crossed home.

"Looks like another big win for the Cardinals," Miranda said. "They've really gotten good." She lay back in the grass. "So, how are things over at the haunted house?"

"Funny you should ask," I told her. "Things are . . . interesting."

"Oh?" She sat up. "Interesting how?"

Out of the corner of my eye, I noticed that

Katherine was listening, too. I ignored her and kept talking to Miranda. I told her about the man on the phone, the family feud, and what had happened upstairs to Susan's things. "Somebody tried to destroy the plans," I told her. "It's like . . . somebody doesn't want the renovations to happen."

"Somebody?" Miranda raised an eyebrow. "Like who?"

You can tell Miranda's in training to be a detective. She listens really closely when you tell her things. If she'd had a notebook with her, she probably would have whipped it out by now to take notes.

"I don't know," I said. "Like, maybe a ghost?" I still didn't want to mention the noises I'd heard. They probably wouldn't believe me, anyway.

Katherine burst out laughing. (See what I mean?) "Oh, come on, Ophelia. You can't be serious!"

Miranda didn't laugh, but she sure looked skeptical. "Ophelia. You don't really believe in ghosts, do you?"

I looked down at the grass and pulled up a couple of shoots. "I don't know. Maybe."

She shook her head. "I'm sure there's a better explanation. I know there are stories about that house, Ophelia, but remember, they're just stories. Don't let yourself get carried away."

"But —"

"Ophelia," Miranda said sternly. "I mean it. Don't start making up ghost stories."

Sometimes Miranda acts like she's my mom or something. Just because she's so much older, she thinks she can order me around. "I changed your diapers," she'll say, like that's supposed to mean something. Olivia probably changed my diapers a million times, but she'd never hold it over me.

"Ghost stories?" That was Helena. She'd come up behind us while we were talking. Her team was up at bat, but she was way down in the order and probably wouldn't get up that inning. "Is there a ghost at the Bascomb place? Cool!"

"There's no ghost, Helena," Katherine said. "Forget it."

"That was a great catch you made," Miranda told her, pulling the old change-the-subject routine.

Helena didn't fall for it. "Thanks. But what about this ghost? Did you see it? What kind of ghost? Is it a poltergeist?"

Helena is crazy about ghost stories. She never gets scared, or if she does she just enjoys it. Want to know the truth? I think the reason Katherine acts so sure that there aren't any ghosts is because she's terrified of them. I remember one time at day camp when the counselors told us a ghost story at nap time. Katherine and I were still sharing a room then, and she didn't sleep for a week. I know because she crawled into bed with me every night and tossed and turned and kept me awake, too.

I'm a little more like Helena. I don't really, really believe in ghosts. I knew there had to be a rational explanation for those noises I'd heard. (Right?) But I do love ghost stories. It's fun to scare yourself a little sometimes. Just a little.

"Can I come over there with you sometime?" asked Helena. "I know all the ways to catch a ghost. If there is one, we can definitely find it."

"I don't know . . ."

"Come on! That girl, Gwen? She seems nice, but she's shy. I bet she needs some friends. If Viola and I came over, she'd probably be really happy."

"Don't beg, Helena," Miranda said, doing the junior-mom thing again.

"I'm not begging! I'm just —"

"Helena," Miranda said warningly.

But Helena had me thinking. What she said made sense. It would be a great way for Gwen to start making friends in her new town. Helena and Viola know everybody. "I'll ask Gwen's mom," I told her. "If she says it's okay, then it's okay."

"Yay!" Helena threw her mitt into the air.

"Helena!" That was her coach calling. "You're on deck!"

"Oops. See you guys. Watch, I'll get a really big hit this time." Helena skipped off to pick out a bat.

Miranda just shook her head at me. "I told you not to get carried away. Now you're getting Helena and Viola involved, too."

"Miranda, it's no big deal. I promise we won't get all crazy. We'll just play Ghostbusters and then they'll forget all about it. Anyway, I think Gwen would be happy if I brought them over."

"Whatever." Miranda shrugged.

She and Katherine and I watched the rest of the game without talking much. I didn't really care. I just relaxed and enjoyed the late-afternoon sun on my back.

Oh — just in case you care: The Cardinals won, eighteen to fifteen.

Chapter Eight

That night, I called Gretchen to ask if I could bring the twins over the next day. She said she'd check with Gwen and Toby and get back to me. Within a half hour, everything was arranged. Helena and Viola and Gwen and Toby would all ride their bikes to school. I'd meet them there, we'd stop by the library (Gwen's request), and then we'd head to the Bascomb place.

I mean, the *Frederick* place. It's hard to break a lifetime habit. People around here will probably call that house the Bascomb place for the next hundred years. Our house is still known as the Turner place, even though no Turners have lived there since 1895!

Anyway, it was all set. As soon as I finished school the next day, I raced over to the elementary school on my bike. I arrived just as the kids were getting out. What a madhouse! I mean, kids were racing all over the playground, yelling at the top of their lungs. Did I act so crazy when I was that age? I spotted Viola in the chaos and waved to her. She pulled her bike from the rack and headed over to join me under the willow tree where we'd agreed to meet. "Hey, Viola," I said.

"Hi." She didn't look too happy.

"What's the matter?" I asked. "Bad day at school?"

She shook her head, staring down at her sneakers.

"Viola?" I asked.

"I hate ghosts," she said finally. "I mean, I guess I'm scared of them. And Helena says —"

"Don't pay attention to her," I interrupted. "It's all just for fun. We won't do anything scary, I promise. We're just going to hang out with Gwen and Toby, get to know them."

Viola still wouldn't look at me.

"Okay?" I asked.

"Okay." I could tell she didn't believe me. I also had a feeling it wasn't just the ghosts that were bothering her. She was probably unsure about going over to a new house with new people. But I knew she'd be fine.

Helena showed up just then, wheeling her bike across the school yard. "Where is everybody?" she asked. "I thought we were meeting right after school."

Could she be any more impatient? "Listen, Helena," I began. "I want you to keep quiet about the ghost thing. We can check things out, but I don't want to scare Gwen and Toby."

"Um, Ophelia?" Helena said. She was giving me this weird look: raised eyebrows, wide eyes, her head cocked sideways. I ignored her.

"I'm not kidding," I told her. "Just keep a lid on it, okay?"

"Lid on what?"

The question came from behind me. I turned around to see Gwen and Toby standing there. Toby was putting his bike helmet on, juggling his backpack and bike at the same time. Gwen, who was already wearing her helmet, was the one who'd asked.

"Oh — um — nothing," I said. Oops. Helena had been trying to let me know they were there. "Here, let me help you with that." I put one hand on Toby's handlebars and reached for his backpack with the other.

"So, are we going to the library?" asked Gwen. Phew. She was moving on. My answer must have satisfied her.

"The library?" wailed Helena.

I whirled around and shot her a look. "I told you," I said. "We're stopping at the library before we go to Gwen and Toby's."

She shrugged. She knew better than to say anything.

We put on our helmets, hopped on our bikes, and rode off toward the library, which isn't far from the elementary school. Our new library is the best. It was built just a couple of years ago. Before that, the library was in the basement of an old church, and even though there weren't that many books, the shelves were overflowing. You could never find anything, and even if you did there was nowhere to sit down and look at it.

The new library is in a big, bright building. It has tons of windows, beautiful oak reading tables, and lots of open space. There still aren't a lot of books, because most of the money was used up on the building. But the library's working on that. The children's room has a carpeted section with cozy built-in seating. It's a comfortable, quiet place to read. I like to hang out there, even though I'm almost too old for the children's room.

When we arrived at the library, Viola headed straight for the fiction area. She is an edacious[12] reader and always has to check out the latest arrivals.

Gwen unzipped her backpack and pulled out three books. She stacked them on the returns desk. The librarian, Mary Jane, smiled at her. "Hi, Gwen. Did you like the Katherine Paterson book?"

Mary Jane's amazing. I don't know how she

---

[12]edacious: having a huge appetite

learns so many names and remembers them all. I mean, Gwen just moved here.

Gwen nodded. "It was great," she said. "Sad, though."

"I know." Mary Jane nodded in agreement.

"So, are you going to get more books?" Helena asked Gwen. "Or can we go?"

Argh! I reached out and gave her a little poke. "Why don't you go find some books of your own?" I suggested.

"Oh, all right." She stomped off toward the nonfiction section.

Toby, meanwhile, grabbed a book about robots and headed for the reading area, after mumbling a comment about how the library in his old town was much better.

Gwen joined Viola at the new-fiction shelf. At first they were both quiet. "Do you like Narnia books?" Gwen finally asked Viola.

Viola nodded. "I like books about magic."

"Me, too. Did you ever read any books by E. Nesbit?"

"Like *The Story of the Amulet*?" Viola was smiling now. "I love those books. They're the best!"

"Aren't we ever going to leave?" That was Helena, holding an armload of books. I checked the titles. *Ghosts I Have Known. Ghosts, Goblins, and Haunted Houses. Thirty Scary Ghost Stories.*

"Chill, Helena," I said. "Go on and sign out your books, then put them away so Gwen doesn't see them."

"Quit ordering me around," Helena said, but she did as I told her. Mary Jane chatted with her while she stamped the books.

Finally, Gwen and Viola came up to the desk, too. Each of them had a stack of books to check out. Curious, I peeked at Gwen's. She'd picked out another Katherine Paterson book, an Edward Eager book called *Half Magic*, and three Nancy Drews.

Hmm. So Gwen liked mysteries. Interesting.

Toby was so lost in his robot book that I had to call him twice before he heard me. He checked it out, and finally we were ready to go.

We got back on our bikes, put on our helmets, and pedaled up West Hill Road to the Bascomb place. Well, we pedaled part of the way. Some of us had to hop off and walk for a while. As you can imagine from its name, the road is hilly. Actually, it's more like one long hill. It's up, up, up all the way. Coming back down is a lot more fun.

Gwen was panting by the time we got to the top. "There aren't any hills like that in Connecticut!" she said.

"You'll get used to it," Viola promised. "I just made it to the top of this hill for the first time last spring. Before that I'd have to push my bike for half of it."

"I'll never get used to it," said Toby. "What good is a bike if you have to *push* it everywhere?"

Helena didn't say anything. She'd ridden up ahead of us the whole way, and by the time we got to the house she was already off her bike, staring up at the turret. There were no trucks in the driveway that afternoon. The workers must have been at another job, or else they'd already quit for the day.

"How about a snack?" I asked as we headed inside.

"I'm not really hungry," Toby said. "I'll be in my room." He slung his backpack over his shoulder and started up the stairs.

"Okay." I'd checked with Gretchen, and she said Toby was allowed to spend as much time as he wanted on the computer. She said she and Mr. Frederick figured it might help him adjust to his new home. "How about the rest of you?" I led the girls into the kitchen and put out some juice, pretzels, and fruit.

Helena was restless, but she managed to control herself. I knew she was dying to get upstairs and check out the attic space. Gwen and Viola kept talking about books; they'd definitely found a common interest.

"I have a whole collection of mysteries," Gwen told Viola. "Want to see? You can borrow some if you want. Come on up to my room."

"Cool!" Viola jumped up from the table. "Is that okay?" she asked me.

"Sure," I said. "Gwen, is it all right if I take Helena up to see the attic? She's curious about what's going on up there." That was no lie.

Gwen shrugged. "Okay." She grabbed Viola's sleeve. "Come on." The two of them ran off toward the stairs.

Helena rolled her eyes. "Finally! Let's go."

I made her wait for a second while I cleaned up the kitchen. Then we headed up to the attic.

"Wow," said Helena, when she saw how the place was torn up. "I bet it never looked like this before. What's that little door?"

"That goes up to the turret," I told her.

She opened her eyes wide. "Can we go up?"

"I guess it's all right." I didn't actually want to go up there at all. That coffin story still haunted me, not to mention those noises I thought I'd heard, or the scary message on the wall. But I didn't want to look chicken in front of Helena. I turned the knob. To my relief, the door was locked again. "Or maybe not. I'll ask Gretchen if we can go up there sometime. I'm sure she'd say yes."

"So, where were those blueprints and the writing on the wall? And where were the pen and the notebook before they got stolen?" Helena prowled around, checking out everything. I'd broken down and told her all the details I could remember about the strange goings-on Susan Duff had mentioned.

"Well, they were on that table," I said, "but it was over there before." I pointed to the opposite side of the room. Now that I looked around, a lot of stuff had been moved and cleaned up since I'd been there last. The blueprints were gone; I figured Susan had taken them away to do them over. And the scrawled message had been painted over.

"What's this?" asked Helena, picking up a scrap of fabric from the floor. It looked like an old linen handkerchief, yellowed with age.

"Let's see," I said. She handed it over. "Wow, check out the fine embroidery." I turned the handkerchief around, looking at the flowers and leaves sewn onto it. The colors were faded, but I could tell they'd once been bright. The stitchwork was perfect, tiny and regular. It must have been sewn by hand, but it looked like a machine had done it.

"Look at that?" Helena pointed to a corner.

I peered closer. "It looks like initials." That part of the handkerchief was a little ragged, but I could still make out the letters. "It says *A. B.* I wonder if this belonged to some long-ago Bascomb?"

"If it did, what's it doing out on the floor?" Helena asked. We stared at each other. Helena had a point. Who — or what — had dropped that handkerchief?

Just then, we heard footsteps on the stairs. We froze. Was it a ghost? Some Bascomb woman, coming back to claim her handkerchief?

"What's up, you guys?" asked Gwen, coming into the room with Viola behind her. Viola's face was a little pale.

Both of us sighed with relief. "We're just — looking around," I said. I glanced down and saw the handkerchief in my hand. It was too late to hide it.

"What's that?" Gwen came over to look at it.

"Just an old handkerchief. It's nothing."

"But look at the initials!" Gwen was excited all of a sudden. "I bet this belonged to a Bascomb. Like, one of my old relatives. Maybe it belongs to the ghost!"

"Ghost? What ghost?" I asked, like I'd never heard the word before.

"You know, the one Mitchell tells stories about. I'm dying to find out more about it. I love ghost stories."

I thought back to the other day. I remembered Gwen sounding scared at the idea of a ghost. But maybe I'd misunderstood.

"Me, too!" Helena jumped right in. "I mean, I

love them, too. And I want to find the ghost. I bet we can, if we work together."

"Cool!" Gwen's face was flushed.

Viola's, on the other hand, was even paler than before.

"Look, it's all just a game," I said, trying to reassure her. So, Gwen was involved after all, along with me and Helena. We were a team now, and I knew we could solve this mystery. All I had to do was try to keep Viola from freaking out. No problem.

That's what I thought, anyway.

Then the door slammed.

The door to the turret. The one that was locked.

You might not believe this, but it's true.

As we were standing there, that door opened all by itself, then suddenly slammed shut with a loud bang.

Chapter Nine

"Ophelia!" Viola grabbed my hand.

"I'm getting out of here," said Helena. She dashed for the stairs. Gwen was right behind her. I guess loving ghost stories doesn't mean you love actual *ghosts*.

All four of us ran downstairs as fast as we could. When we got to the bottom of the stairs, we kept right on going, out the front door. I think everyone felt the same way I did: I *had* to get out of that house. I was freaking out, I admit it. This time, I couldn't talk myself out of it, like I'd done with the other noises I'd heard. This time, I wasn't alone. There were four of us, and we'd all seen and heard the same thing.

We stood under a bright red maple tree, panting.

"That — that door!" Gwen gasped. "It slammed —"

"All by itself!" Helena added.

"I saw it," Viola agreed. She was rubbing her hands together. "I saw it and I heard it and I don't even want to *think* about it."

Viola was really and truly scared. We all were.

But suddenly I realized something. It was time for me to take control of the situation. After all, I was the baby-sitter. I couldn't let the girls work themselves into a total panic. "Look," I said. "There has to be some explanation. We'll figure it out. Meanwhile, let's try to forget about it for a little while. It's a beautiful day. Let's —" I glanced around, hoping for inspiration. "Let's gather some of these leaves. We can iron them between sheets of wax paper for window decorations."

The idea was kind of lame, but it worked. I think the girls were ready to be distracted. We spent the rest of the afternoon wandering around picking up the prettiest leaves we could find, sorting them into piles, and thinking about other crafts projects we could use them for.

After that day, I didn't want to think about ghosts for a while. Fortunately, there was something else for me to obsess about.

The literary magazine.

Chapter Ten

There was another meeting after school on Thursday. (Luckily, I didn't have to sit for the Fredericks that day.) Ms. Cooper had put seven chairs in a circle, but once the meeting started we had to widen the circle and add a bunch more chairs. There were at least twenty people there!

"Well, this is encouraging," Ms. Cooper said, looking around the circle. "I'm so glad that interest in the magazine is growing."

Little did she know. I glared at Katherine, across the circle from me. Interest, ha. Most of the newcomers were only interested in one thing, and that thing had a long blond braid and was wearing a baby-blue tee that said ANGEL across the chest in silver glitter.

In other words, Katherine's followers had followed her — straight to Ms. Cooper's room. Almost all the newcomers were male.

I was disgusted. I knew those boys. They weren't interested in poetry or fiction. Most of them probably never read anything deeper than the box scores in the sports section. Katherine was just bringing in votes so that when the time came, she'd be named editor.

I turned to Zoe and gave her a little eye roll. She returned it. She knew what was up.

You might be wondering about Zoe being there, since I know I've made it sound like she's only interested in sports. You might even think I was up to the same tricks as my sister, bringing people to the meeting just so they'd support me. Well, you'd be wrong. True, I'd had to promise to buy Zoe a maple creemee[13] after the meeting, but that wasn't the only reason she had come. It just so happened that her track practice was canceled because big thunderstorms were in the forecast, and Zoe was looking for something to do. Coming to this meeting probably wouldn't have been her first choice, I admit that. But she came of her own free will.

So did Emma, who was sitting on my other side.

I know, it doesn't look good. But they're my friends, and they want to support me. Is that so wrong?

"Well," said Ms. Cooper, looking around the circle, "I guess the first thing on the agenda for today is to pick —"

"I nominate Katherine!" yelled out Michael Stamper.

Ms. Cooper raised her eyebrows. "Well, I'm sure

---

[13]maple creemee: a Vermont favorite. Soft ice cream, flavored with real maple syrup

you do." I thought I saw her smile. "But I'm not sure that *Katherine* would make a good name for a literary magazine. That's what I was about to suggest that we talk about today: a name."

"Oh." Michael was blushing.

Katherine smiled at him from across the circle. I even saw her nictitating[14] at him.

Michael blushed an even deeper red.

"I know some of you are eager to pick an editor," she said, "but I think there are other decisions that need to come first." She looked serious for a moment. "I want to add that this is not a popularity contest. Whoever we pick for editor will be picked on his or her own merits, not on how much we all admire him or her."

I hate when teachers use that "not a popularity contest" line. The truth is, most things in middle school *are* a popularity contest. It's pointless to pretend they're not. But Ms. Cooper meant what she said. She really believed we'd elect an editor who would be best for the magazine. I could only hope she was right.

The room was quiet for a second. Then Martha cleared her throat. "I can take notes again," she offered, holding up her notebook.

"That would be great," Ms. Cooper said.

[14]nictitating: winking

82

"Thanks, Martha. But maybe you could write on the blackboard, so we can all see?"

Martha jumped up and stood by the blackboard, ready to write.

"Okay, people, let's brainstorm." Ms. Cooper sat back and folded her arms.

"How about *The U-28 Literary Magazine*?" That was Ben Thomas. He's never been too imaginative.

Everybody groaned.

Ms. Cooper held up her hands. "No comments, please. Remember, this is brainstorming. Every idea gets heard. Go ahead and write that down, Martha."

Martha wrote it down.

"I was thinking maybe *Echoes* would be a good name," Sally said.

Nobody groaned. But nobody agreed. They all probably thought the same thing I did. *Echoes* was okay but nothing special.

Martha wrote the name on the board.

"I was picturing it with a small *e*." Sally isn't shy about saying what she thinks.

Martha erased the big *E* and put in a small one. The name didn't look any more interesting.

There was a pause. "Anybody else?" Ms. Cooper sounded a little anxious. I couldn't blame her. So far, there wasn't a winner.

"*Galaxy Twenty-eight!*" called out Matthew.

Ew. That sounded like a bad science-fiction

movie. It figured Matthew would come up with something like that. I could tell people were trying hard not to make Ms. Cooper mad by groaning.

Martha didn't even pause. She wrote that name right underneath *echoes.*

Katherine spoke up next. "What about something that refers to books?" she asked. "Like *Folio.*"

"Yeah!" That was Justin Tanaka. "I like it!" He looked at Katherine for approval of his approval.

Did Justin even know what a folio was? I happen to know that it's a term for a set of book pages. I was tempted to expose him by asking him what the word meant.

Actually, Katherine's idea was pretty good. But I wasn't about to say so. Or should I? Maybe it would make me look open and tolerant. Then I saw the look Ms. Cooper was giving Justin, and I decided to keep my mouth shut. Instead, I just smiled and nodded as I watched Martha add the name to her list.

A few more names were shouted out. Dave Stewart offered *Buzzbomb* and Sam Winston suggested *Ollie.* (That's a skateboard term, in case you don't know.) Yes, you guessed it: Both Dave and Sam were F.O.K.'s.[15]

Martha wrote everything down. Then she turned from the blackboard. "I have one," she of-

[15]F.O.K.'s: Friends Of Katherine

fered. "I was thinking that a name from mythology might be good. Like, maybe *Pegasus*?"

Hey. That was good. The image of a winged horse was perfect.

"Nice," said Ms. Cooper.

Martha smiled and ducked her head, blushing.

"Don't forget to write it down," Ms. Cooper added. "Anybody else?"

Why hadn't I thought about this before I'd come to the meeting? I knew I could have come up with a perfect name, if I'd just given it some time. But no, I had to get all caught up in this ghost thing. I thought as hard as I could.

Then, "How about — how about *Quintessence*?" I called out, before I could stop myself.

Zoe stared at me with a puzzled look on her face. But Ms. Cooper laughed. "Great," she said.

Wow. That felt good.

Ms. Cooper must have noticed a few blank looks around the circle. "Want to explain what it means?" she asked.

Martha had already written it down, spelling it perfectly. "It's, like, the essence of something. The perfect example. Like" — I fished desperately — "Zoe is the quintessential goalie."

Everybody knew that Zoe rarely lets a soccer ball into the goal. They all laughed. Zoe gave me a little punch on the arm, like I'd embarrassed her. But she was smiling.

"That's excellent," said Bradley White. "What a cool word." He looked straight at me when he said that and smiled. Bradley has these huge brown eyes, and his smile is crooked and interesting. My stomach did a little flip. Not that I like Bradley. I mean, I like him fine. But I don't *like him* like him. I don't think.

"*Quintessence*," Katherine said, as if she were trying out the word. "It's good."

Was she agreeing with my suggestion to make herself look good? I checked her expression. No. Katherine was being sincere. She really did like my idea!

So, here's the funny thing. I'll spare you the suspense: My suggestion won. The magazine's going to be called *Quintessence*.

And why, you may ask, did my idea win?

Was it because it was the best name? I don't think so. I think there were other good ideas. If it came down to a vote, I might have voted for Martha's suggestion. *Pegasus* would have been an excellent name.

But it didn't come down to a vote. We decided by Ms. Cooper's favorite method, consensus. That's where everybody has to come to an agreement by talking things through. It's not a quick process. But, according to Ms. Cooper, it's the best.

Everybody gets to voice an opinion and nobody feels left out. You keep working on it until everybody agrees.

In this case, consensus came quickly. Why? Easy. Because Katherine said she liked my name best. That meant that all the boys in the room liked it best, too. And, actually, most of the girls. (Katherine's not just popular with boys. Everybody likes her.) In fact, I think the only person who wasn't so sure was Sally. She still liked *echoes.*

Oh, and Billy Smallwood wasn't crazy about it, either. "As an artist," he said, "I have to think about the visuals. How do you illustrate 'quintessence'? I mean, what's our logo going to look like?"

"You're creative enough to come up with something," Katherine told him.

That shut Billy up in a hurry.

In the end, Sally came around. Somebody — I think it was Martha — suggested that one of the sections inside the magazine could be called *echoes.*

"The poetry section?" Sally asked. She wasn't going to give in easily.

"Why not?" Ms. Cooper obviously thought the suggestion was a good one, and the rest of us agreed.

So, here's the word of the day: irony[16].

---

[16]irony: a difference between what you expect and what really happens

Katherine and I were in a bitter battle to become editor of the magazine. We'd each brought in our forces to support us. So it was ironic that she — and her forces — ended up making me look so good.

By the time we broke up that day, everybody was exhausted. Brainstorming and consensus-building are tiring! Ms. Cooper reminded us that we had a lot more to decide before we could get to work on the magazine. "We'll keep meeting once or twice a week until we work out all the details," she said as we got ready to go. "I'm as excited as the rest of you about . . ." She paused. "*Quintessence.*"

She looked right at me and smiled.

I felt — how did I feel? I should be able to describe it, but I can't. I know it sounds like a cliché, but at that second it really felt like time stood still. As I stood there, grinning back at Ms. Cooper (I probably looked like a total idiot), I couldn't hear anything but her voice or see anything but her smile. The word *quintessence* seemed to echo all over the room. All I can say is this: That had to be one of the best moments of my middle-school career.

Chapter Eleven

"Quintessence?" Poppy nodded. "Excellent, Ophelia. That's my sesquipedalian[17] daughter. It has a real ring to it. I like it."

At dinner that night, I could hardly wait for my turn so I could tell about what had happened at the meeting. Poppy was obviously impressed. Mom liked the name, too. "It's different," she said. "My high-school literary magazine was called *echoes*, with a small *e*. I always thought that was a little — well, blah."

Katherine smiled at me across the table and I smiled back before I remembered that we were rivals and that I was mad at her. Actually, I wasn't feeling so angry anymore. How could I, after she'd supported me in the meeting? But don't worry; I wasn't backing down. I still wanted to be editor, and I was still prepared to fight for the position.

"I never get to name anything," Juliet complained. "Our school's newspaper already has a dumb name, and I was too young to help when we

[17]sesquipedalian: liking to use long words

got our pets. Can we get another animal, so I can name it?"

"No." Mom didn't even pretend to consider it. "You can name the trees in the backyard, but we're not getting any more animals, and that's final."

"I was just asking." Juliet reached out for the platter of chicken and helped herself to seconds. "Forget it, okay?"

"We already have," Poppy said, smiling at her. "More potatoes?"

Mom pushed back her chair. "Sorry to eat and run, but if I don't get going I'll be late for our special recorder group rehearsal."

I knew she'd be seeing Mr. Frederick — Michael — there. Hopefully, he wouldn't mention anything about a possible ghost. Mom wouldn't like it much if she knew Helena and Viola and I were chasing ghosts. She thinks that sort of thing is pointless.

She may be right. In a way, I almost hope she is. I mean, if it really was a ghost slamming that door — ! But somehow, I couldn't wait to get back to the Bascomb place to find out more.

Neither could Helena. She barged into the bathroom that night when I was in there checking my bangs in the mirror. They were already growing in a little. They didn't look quite as dorky as they had a few days ago.

"So, we have a whole plan for tomorrow," she told me, joining me at the mirror and making a fish face at herself.

"'We' who?" I asked.

"Gwen and me. And Viola, too."

"And what are you all planning?" This was news to me.

"A real investigation. We're going to figure out what's going on up there in the attic."

"So that means you want to come over there with me tomorrow?" I asked. I was sitting Friday afternoon and evening.

She nodded.

"I'll check with Gwen's mom."

"You don't have to. Gwen already asked, and it's fine. We're even invited for dinner."

Oh. "And is Viola all right with your plans?"

"Kind of. She says she's decided not to believe in ghosts. But she's still curious about what's happening."

I was, too. That's why I was just as glad nobody wanted to stop at the library the next day after school. We just pedaled — and walked — our bikes up the hill as fast as possible. Toby didn't seem the least bit interested in our ghost-busting plans. When we arrived at the house, he grabbed a big handful of Fig Newtons and a couple of apples and disappeared upstairs.

The rest of us — Gwen, Helena, Viola, and me — gathered around the kitchen table to look at a diagram Gwen had made. I'd put out some cheese and crackers for a snack, but nobody was eating. "See, this shows how the rooms used to look and how they look now," Gwen said, pointing out the dotted lines that showed walls that no longer existed. "I copied this part from the blueprints."

This is what Gwen's diagram looked like:

"What are the X's for?" I asked.

"Those are to show where different things happened," Gwen explained. "Like, this X is for that writing on the wall, and this one's where Susan Duff left her notebook and pen. She still hasn't found them, by the way. I asked her last night."

"And this X?" I asked.

"That's for the door that slammed. And this one" — she pointed to another — "is for that handkerchief you found."

"I thought so." I wondered where I would put X's for the footsteps and the crying sounds I'd heard. I knew I should tell them about that, but I didn't want to scare Viola.

"This is so cool, Gwen. But I want to see the real thing. Let's go upstairs now!" Helena was impatient.

"We can't," I told her. "Didn't you see the truck

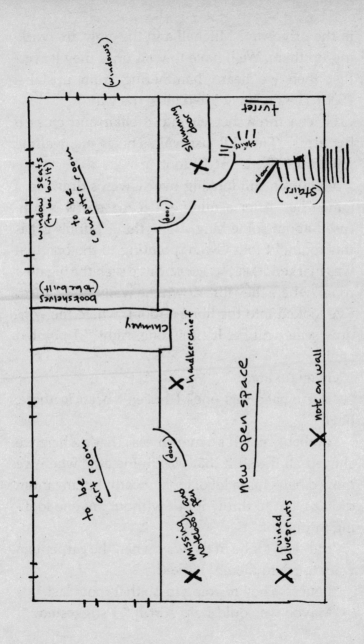

in the driveway? Mitchell and the crew are working up there. We'll have to wait until they leave." Just then we heard hammering from upstairs. "See? They're busy. We'd be in the way."

Helena threw herself into a chair and crossed her arms. "Fine. I'll just wait. This is me, waiting patiently." She tapped a foot.

Viola was still looking over Gwen's drawing. I joined her. After a minute, I realized I was confused about something. "One thing I don't get is this room," I told Gwen, pointing to the one that was marked TO BE ART ROOM. "I've seen the big new room, where they tore down the walls, and I guess I've looked into the library room, where the window seats will be. It's this one, right?" I pointed again.

Gwen nodded.

"But what's this one? I haven't been in there, have I?"

"Probably not. It's a huge mess. That's where we shoved all the stuff that was in the attic when we moved here. Just a lot of junk, mostly, but my mom didn't want to throw it out without anyone looking through it."

"But won't it be in the way when the carpenters want to get in there?" I asked.

"I guess. They're going to do that room last."

"Maybe we could help sort it," I suggested. "I

love looking through old stuff." During garage-sale season, my family calls me "the junk-hound." I can scope out a yard sale in no time flat, picking out all the good buys and useful things and avoiding the garbage that some people try to sell. You should see the bargains I've found! The chairs in our study, for example. I got those for five bucks apiece at the church's annual rummage sale. In my mind, "valuable junk" is no oxymoron.[18]

"I bet my mom would love that," Gwen said. "We could start today!"

I wasn't sure we should start without asking Gretchen first. But I was getting that itchy, "gotta check it out" feeling I get when I see yard-sale signs. The temptation was too much for me. "We could even go up there now, I suppose," I said. "Since they're not working in that room yet." I was practically on my way upstairs already. But then the phone rang.

Gwen and I looked at each other.

"I guess we should just let the machine pick up again," I said.

She shrugged. "He's been calling every day," she said.

"Who?" asked Helena.

---

[18]oxymoron: a phrase that includes two contradictory words: pretty ugly, seriously funny, bittersweet

I held up a hand. "Shhh. Wait."

We listened as the machine clicked on and Graham Bascomb's voice came over the speaker. "This is Graham Bascomb again," he said. "I'm calling to arrange a time to visit. And I'm going to keep calling until we come to an agreement. So you might as well talk to me one of these days."

Click.

"Who was that?" Viola asked. "Did he say Bascomb?"

Gwen and I took turns explaining about the long-lost Bascomb relative who said he had a claim on the house. Viola was listening carefully. She's good at that.

"Where does he live?" she asked when we were done.

Gwen shrugged. "Don't know."

"We can find out," Viola said. Before I could stop her, she surprised me by jumping up, picking up the phone, and punching in some numbers. She listened for a moment and scribbled something down on the pad next to the answering machine. Then she turned to us.

"He's in Vermont," she said. "In fact, he's probably only a few miles away."

"What?" I reached for the pad, and she handed it to me. Viola had written down a phone number. And the number not only had the same area code as ours, it had the same first three numbers as Olivia's. That meant Graham Bascomb was calling from Burlington.

"How did you do that?" asked Gwen.

"Easy," Viola told her. "There's a code that lets you know who called you last. Katherine does it all the time when she thinks Billy Smallwood called."

"And I think it costs something, too," I informed her. "You shouldn't have done it without checking with Gwen's mom." Still, it was interesting to know that Graham Bascomb was in the area. This whole time I had assumed he was far away, like in New Jersey or something.

"Are we going to talk about this Bascomb dude all day?" Helena asked. "Or are we going to check things out upstairs?"

"I vote for upstairs!" Gwen jumped up. "Let's go."

"That okay with you?" I asked Viola. I knew she was still a little nervous about the ghost thing.

"Sure." She followed us upstairs, but not, I noticed, before she'd torn off the piece of paper with Graham Bascomb's number on it and put it in her pocket.

"Hey." Mitchell looked up and smiled at us as we came into the big, open room. "Up here for some ghost-busting?"

"We're just looking around," Gwen said.

"Is that okay?" I asked. "We were going to go in that room." I pointed to a closed door at the end of the hall.

"That's the popular room today," Mitchell said. "Toby was in there just now. And the guy who was here earlier was, too."

"Guy?" Gwen asked. "What guy?"

"I think he works for Susan. Tall blond guy with a mustache. He said he needed to check out a few things."

Mitchell sounded vague. He was picking out a piece of wood from a big pile of lumber. Lori and Steve were over by one of the windows, taking measurements. Nobody seemed to care what we were up to.

Gwen led us down the hall and opened the door. "See what I mean?" she asked, peering inside. "It's a total mess."

We crowded in behind her. Gwen was right. The room was crammed full of dusty furniture, old trunks, and piles of books and papers. "Wow." It was a little overwhelming, even for a junk-hound like me.

"Looks like a perfect place for a ghost to live," Helena said in a hushed voice.

Viola didn't say anything.

"Well?" Gwen asked.

"Let's go in." I couldn't resist. "I mean, we'll just look around a little, right? No big deal." I pushed the door open a little more and stepped inside. The others followed me. Dust rose up as I walked through the room, even though I hadn't touched anything yet. Even the windows were dusty, so the light was filtered and weak. I found a path through the broken-down chairs and old bureaus with cracked and peeling paint. We were quiet as we looked around.

Then there was a crash.

"Did you see that?" Helena asked, pointing. "That picture frame just, like, *flew* off the wall. That's one of the first signs of a poltergeist!"

"What?" Viola's voice was all trembly.

"Don't listen to her, Viola," I said. "It just fell because we were all walking around in here and shaking things up."

"If that's what you want to believe," Helena said in a low voice.

I tried to forget the poltergeist comment as we walked deeper into the jam-packed room. "Huh!" I said, jumping as I nearly ran into an old dressmaker's dummy. It wasn't that I was scared by it; I was just — surprised.

Helena giggled. Then she gasped. "Check out this old trunk," she said. She stood before an ancient-looking trunk, black beneath the dust and trimmed with tarnished brass. "Cool." She bent to open it.

"It's probably —" Gwen began.

The trunk popped open.

"Locked," Gwen finished. "Or not."

We all crowded around to look inside. The trunk was full of neatly folded old clothes. I mean *extremely* old. Antique. Most of them were black, like the dress Helena pulled out. It was full-length, with yellowed lace trim at the neck and wrists. "I wonder who wore this."

"Probably the same person who wrote in this," Viola answered in a very quiet voice. She reached into the trunk and pulled out an old, leather-bound book. *Diary*, it said on the front, in faded gold script.

"Wow," Gwen breathed. "Can I see?"

A little reluctantly, Viola handed over the book.

Gwen opened the little clasp. "It's not locked." The leather cracked as she held the book, and flakes of it dropped off onto the floor. She opened the book to its first page. "'My diary for 1877,'" she read. "'Abigail Bascomb, age fifteen.'"

Chapter Twelve

We stared at the book in Gwen's hands.

"Wow." Helena's voice was quiet. "That is so cool."

Gwen looked a little pale. "It's a real diary," she said. "Of a real girl, from the past."

"Abigail Bascomb," Viola said softly. "She must have lived in this house."

"So what are we waiting for?" Helena asked. "Aren't we going to read it?"

"Read it?" Gwen was startled. "But it's — it's somebody's diary. That's private."

Ha. You can tell Gwen doesn't have six sisters. I've tried keeping a journal, but I've never been able to find a hiding place that one of my nosy siblings couldn't find. There are no secrets in the Parker household.

"Private?" Helena stared at Gwen. "Come on! She's probably been dead for at least" — she did some quick math in her head — "seventy-five years!"

"So?" Gwen stared back. "It's still private. Would you want somebody reading your diary, even after you died?"

Helena shrugged. "Why not? It's their problem if they want to be bored to death. All my diary ever says is, 'Went to school. Played soccer. We won. Ate dinner. Bed.' Why would I care if anyone saw that?"

"But we don't know what Abigail wrote about." Gwen was holding the diary close to her chest.

"I agree with Helena."

That was Viola. Gwen turned to her. "Really?"

Viola nodded. "I mean, it's true that diaries are private. But it's also true that she's dead, and nothing can hurt her. It's not like we're going to tell anyone her secrets. We could even swear not to."

"Like, take a vow?" Gwen was wavering.

"Right. We can promise that we'll never talk about anything we read." Viola was really getting into it.

"What do you think?" Gwen asked me.

"I think I'm dying to know what's in that book." I had to be honest. I could see Gwen's point, but still. Wouldn't you want to read the diary? Wouldn't anyone?

Gwen closed the lid of the trunk and sat down on it. "So I guess I'm the only one who thinks we shouldn't."

The rest of us were quiet.

"It's up to you," I said. "I mean, this is your

102

house. And your attic. The diary belongs to your family." I held my breath as I waited to see what she'd say. Helena and Viola were also very still.

"Well" — she looked down at the book in her hand — "I guess it's kind of educational. It would be good to learn about the family that used to live here. My parents would probably think so."

Yikes. Parents. I didn't want to go there. If Gwen decided we should ask her parents, who knew how long we'd have to wait! "I'm sure they would," I agreed quickly, even though I wasn't sure at all. I have no excuse. I just really, really wanted to read that book!

"So, all right." Gwen looked around at us. "Let's take a vow." She raised her right hand, and we all copied her. "I swear," she began.

"I swear," we echoed solemnly.

Gwen suddenly looked blank.

"How about 'that I will never, ever talk about the secrets I read in this book'?" Helena suggested.

"That's great! Let's say that." Gwen nodded eagerly.

Keeping our hands up, we repeated what Helena had said.

"Okay." Gwen looked down at the book, which she was holding in both hands, and took a deep breath. Then she shoved it into my hands. "You read."

"Sure?"

"Sure."

She moved over on the trunk to make room. I sat down next to her, and Helena and Viola leaned over my shoulder. There wasn't a whole lot of light in the room, so I had to strain a bit to make out the faded black script. "'I, Abigail Elizabeth Bascomb, do now begin this book,'" I began. "'Whoever may come across it someday in the far future, please judge me not by my abominable hand —'"

"What?" Helena looked confused. "I thought only snowmen were abominable."

"I think she means her handwriting is terrible," I said. "Which it isn't, really. It's old-fashioned and hard to read, but it's still a whole lot better than mine."

"Wait a minute!" Gwen held up a hand. "What's that noise?"

We all fell silent for a moment, but the room was quiet.

"What noise?" asked Helena.

Gwen looked a little pale. "Nothing, I guess," she said. "I just — I thought I heard someone crying."

I stared at her. So she'd heard it, too.

"Crying?" asked Viola.

Gwen shook her head. "Never mind. I must have imagined it."

We were quiet for another second.

"Okay, okay, let's get back to the diary," demanded Helena.

I shook off my shivers and went back to reading. "'— or by my imperfect spelling and grammar. I do my best, but as Father often tells me, I will never be a scholar.'"

"I wonder what her father's name was? Maybe my mom has heard of him. Or of Abigail," Gwen mused.

"Look, it's all written down," I said. "She has a family tree here." I showed Gwen the book. On the second page, Abigail had made a chart of her whole family, noting their birth dates and relationships. "See, her father's name was Isaiah." I pointed. "And her mother's was Sarah. She had two sisters, named Emily and Hannah. Let's see." I took a closer look at the birth dates. "Both of them were younger. So Abigail was the oldest. Oh, and there was a son, too. Named Joseph. He died, though. When he was — let's see — five years old."

"He died?" Viola was shocked.

"People died a lot younger then," I said. "And a lot more kids and babies died than they do now." I'd done a project once for social studies, looking at headstones in the old cemetery on Dodge Road. I remember being amazed at how many children were buried there.

"I think maybe my grandmother's aunt was named Emily," Gwen said. "I'm not sure, though."

"If that's right, then Abigail would be related to you somehow," I said. "Like, she'd be your second cousin twice removed or something." Not that I had any idea what that actually meant.

Gwen was nodding. "Maybe. Anyway, keep going."

"Okay." I turned the page carefully, afraid that the book would disintegrate in my hands. "The diary starts on January first. She must have gotten it as a Christmas present." I read slowly. I was still having a hard time with Abigail's writing.

January 1, 1877

Snow last night, and plenty of it. The drifts are as high as Father's shoulders! When I woke up, the sun was shining just as hard as it ever could. It looked so beautiful outside that I could not resist putting on my cloak and running out to see and feel it. Mother was furious and said I would catch my death. In Father's opinion, the only thing for a girl to do when it snows this hard is to stay indoors and sew or cook. So sew and cook we did, until I nearly died of boredom. What a waste of this clean, crisp day.

"I know exactly how she felt," breathed Viola. "Last winter when we had that blizzard, I was dying to go out and play, but Mom made me finish my book report. Then we had a snow day anyway!"

"She sounds just like a regular girl," I agreed. "Like she could be a friend of ours." Which was cool, but also slightly spooky.

"Read some more!" Helena demanded.

I turned the page.

January 2

More snow. More sewing and cooking. I slipped outside once today, for but ten minutes. The rest of the day passed as did yesterday. Neither Hannah nor Emily seem to mind. I most certainly do mind. If only I'd been born a boy! Cousin Samuel has undoubtedly spent both days doing as he wishes, playing in the bountiful drifts and coming inside only when he is too tired and cold. Or perhaps he has had to help Uncle Peter with some chores, but I would not mind that. I would not mind any occupation that allowed me to work outdoors instead of forcing me to sit quietly and spend my energy on the most tedious and repetitive tasks.

Poor Abigail. This was way, way before girl power. "Imagine being a girl back then." I put the book down in my lap for a moment. "I mean, Helena, you wouldn't be playing soccer or softball, that's for sure."

"I wouldn't be sewing, either," she insisted.

"Oh, yes, you would. You wouldn't have any choice."

"Maybe Abigail convinced her mother that she could do other things," Viola suggested.

"Yeah! Skip ahead a little." Gwen reached over and flipped a few pages. "We can go back later and read all the entries. I want to find out what happened when spring came."

I ran my finger down the page she'd flipped to. "This entry is from May sixteenth."

"Cool. Read it!"

"'More arguments with Mother and Father,'" I began.

"Uh-oh," said Helena.

I have refused to put up my hair as Mother says a young lady must. It's too much fuss! The braids I have been wearing all my life are so simple. Why must I change? Father also says I must. But I won't. I won't.

I stopped. "Wow! She's a real rebel."

Helena agreed. "She's way cool."

"Read one from the summer!" Viola nudged my arm.

"Okay." I flipped forward. "How about this one, from July eighteenth?" I started reading. "'This morning was glorious. I slipped out at dawn to feel the cool dew on my feet. I danced through the grass, feeling the breeze ruffle my nightdress —'"

"Oh, no!" Viola said. "Her parents aren't going to like that. What if she gets caught?"

"She did," I said, reading ahead a little. "Oh, boy. She's in trouble now. She's been sent to her room without supper."

"She was grounded?" Helena asked.

"Worse than that," I said, flipping ahead some more. I was reading to myself quickly. And suddenly, I felt a little sick to my stomach. "It sounds like she ended up being grounded permanently."

"What do you mean?" Viola was upset.

I was upset, too. I'd already decided to like this Abigail Elizabeth Bascomb. And now I was finding out that she ended up spending most of her fifteenth year in this very attic.

I almost didn't want to tell the others. I knew it would upset them, maybe even scare them. But I couldn't lie, either. "The thing is," I said, "the way she acted was really different for those days. They thought she was kind of crazy."

"So? Did they get her some therapy?" You could tell Gwen was from Connecticut.

I shook my head. "That's not how things worked back then." I picked a selection from September and read out loud.

Father says I am lucky. Some girls would be sent to the asylum if they behaved as I have done. But I may live here, at home. Only I am not fit for company. I must be hidden away so as not to offend the preacher's wife or any other stranger who visits.

"What?" Helena was indignant. "What's an asylum? And what do they care what the preacher's wife thinks?"

"An asylum is like a mental hospital."

Helena frowned. "But she wasn't crazy!"

"Of course she wasn't. But in those days she must have seemed pretty far-out. And this is a small town. If word got around that their daughter was insane, I guess the Bascombs might have had a hard time." It didn't make sense to me, either.

"So they made her stay up in the attic?" Gwen stared down at the book. "*That's* insane."

"I don't think they exactly locked her in," I said, trying to calm everybody down. "I think they just — kept her up here." I looked around at the gloomy room. "It was probably a lot more comfortable than this."

"That's horrible!" Viola cried. "Poor Abigail. All she wanted was some freedom. And instead she got stuck up here."

It *was* pretty horrible. I almost wished we hadn't started reading. I hated to think of that cool, rebellious girl sitting in this dark, stuffy room. "Maybe it didn't go on for long," I said, flipping ahead again. "Let's try another entry." I found one for November third. "'I am so intolerably lonely and bored,'" I read. "'I think I may go mad and prove Father and Mother right after all. This garret seems smaller each day, and as the winter comes on and light fades I can barely see to do my detested needlework. . . .'"

I stopped reading. First of all, it was too depressing. Second, I suddenly realized that *our* light was fading, too. We must have been up there for hours. I hadn't heard hammering for a long time; Mitchell and the rest of the carpenters must have packed up and gone home already. It was probably way past time for dinner. Toby must be starving!

"We'd better stop," I said. "It's getting late."

"No!" wailed Gwen. "We have to find out what happened to her."

"We will," I told her. No way was I going to give up on Abigail and leave her in that attic. "But not

111

now. Anyway, I can't even see to read anymore." I got up and stretched. "Come on, you guys. Let's take a break. I'll make us some supper and —"

Suddenly, there was the sound of running footsteps. We all heard it. Then, another sound.

Slam!

That unmistakable sound. We'd all heard it before, but it still made us jump. The door slammed once, twice, three times. Each slam sounded louder and angrier than the one before. I thought of that message painted on the wall: GO AWAY NOW! There was no question that somebody — or some-*thing* didn't want us here.

Viola looked up at me. "Is it the ghost?" she asked, her voice shaking.

I couldn't stand to see her so scared. I reached out to touch her shoulder. "No," I said. "I mean — maybe it's Mitchell or somebody." I raised my voice.

"M-Mitchell?" It had to be him. He must be working late, still hammering. Or maybe he was joking around, pretending to be the ghost.

There was no answer.

I tiptoed to the door, opened it, and looked out. It wasn't quite as dark in the big, open area, and I could see that it was empty. No Mitchell. Nobody else.

At least, nobody else visible.

Nobody else alive.

Chapter Thirteen

I knew better.

I mean, I really don't believe in ghosts.

But I couldn't help thinking that the spirit of Abigail Elizabeth Bascomb was nearby.

And she didn't seem happy.

Chapter Fourteen

I closed the door and turned to face the others. They were frozen in place.

"Is — is somebody out there?" Gwen asked.

I shook my head.

"Oh, man," Helena moaned.

Viola was obviously speechless. I rubbed her shoulder. "It's okay," I said, hoping I sounded reassuring.

She frowned. "I know." Her face was pale, but her voice was steady. "You guys think that's a ghost. But I know it's not. There's no such thing as ghosts."

"Fine," said Helena. "If you're so sure, why don't you go out there?"

"We all have to go out there," I told her. "We can't stay in this room forever."

"I wish I could," Gwen said under her breath.

"Okay, then. Well, we'd better head downstairs and get dinner going," I said brightly and a little louder than was necessary. I wanted whoever — or whatever — was slamming those doors to hear me and know we were leaving.

Then I opened the door again and peeked out,

just like I had moments ago. "Oh!" I gasped. I couldn't help myself.

"What? What?" Viola asked.

"It's nothing," I said. But there was no way I could hide it from her. "Well, not nothing exactly. It's just a note."

Another scrawled message on the wall, to be exact.

This time, it was in red paint.

LEAVE THIS PLA

The message was unfinished, as if the writer had been interrupted. As if the writer had heard someone say something about how they were going to "head downstairs and get dinner going." As if the writer had been standing right outside the door, just moments ago.

Yikes.

What could I do? I hurried the girls out of the attic, trying not to give them too much time to stare at the scary, dripping letters. There was something about that bloodred paint that gave me chills.

As we passed Toby's room on the way downstairs, I poked my head in to tell him we'd be eating soon. Down in the kitchen, I got busy making dinner. Gretchen had left some chili in the fridge, so I heated that up. I also steamed some broccoli, even though she'd warned me that it was unlikely that Gwen or Toby would eat it. Soon, I felt a little calmer. It helped to be doing normal, everyday things like cutting up vegetables.

While I cooked, Gwen and the twins sat at the kitchen table, talking about what had happened in the attic.

"It had to be a ghost!" said Gwen.

"Not just any ghost, either," Helena agreed. "That was Abigail Elizabeth Bascomb herself." She was so sure of herself now that we were downstairs in the bright, warm kitchen where doors did not slam all by themselves.

"If that's what you guys want to think, fine." Viola crossed her arms. "But I don't believe in ghosts. There has to be some other explanation."

Good for Viola.

"Like what?" Gwen asked. "Why else would those noises be happening?"

I knew just what Viola was getting at. "Well, if you think about it," I said slowly, "if someone didn't want those renovations to be happening — if they didn't want your family to be living here — they might pretend to be a ghost."

Viola nodded. "Exactly."

"That's ridiculous!" said Helena.

"Think about it some more," I suggested. "Like, somebody might be trying to scare the Fredericks away from this house."

"Somebody — like Graham Bascomb?" Gwen said slowly.

"Exactly," Viola said again, triumphantly.

"He *is* in the area," I said. "We found that out when we traced his call."

"But —" Helena didn't want to let go of her ghost. "But how could he get into the attic without anyone seeing him? And why would he steal a pen?"

"Or leave a handkerchief," Gwen added. Then she clapped a hand over her mouth. Her eyes were round. "The handkerchief! Remember what the initials were?"

I thought for a second. "A. B., right?" Then it hit me. "Abigail Bascomb!"

"See?" Helena said. "Where would Graham Bascomb get that?" She looked smug.

Helena really wanted there to be a ghost upstairs, and she wasn't about to give up on the idea. Gwen wasn't so sure, and neither was I.

"Who says it's really her handkerchief?" I asked. "I mean, her actual initials are A.E.B., and if she had done the embroidery she probably would have put them all in. So that doesn't prove anything. Listen, Helena. You can think whatever you want. But Viola's right. There could be other explanations, and we should check them all out."

"Explanations?" Helena asked. "So far, all I've heard is one, besides Abigail."

"We should make a list," I said. "Of all the possible suspects. That's how you start an investigation."

Gwen jumped up and grabbed a pad and pen from the little desk near the kitchen phone. The pad said THINGS TO REMEMBER on top and had a picture of a finger with string tied around it. Does anybody actually do that? She sat back down and started writing. "'Possible Suspects,'" she read out loud when she was done. "So, who should we put down?"

"Abigail Elizabeth Bascomb." Helena crossed her arms and grinned. "She's my only suspect."

"Okay," Gwen said, writing it down. "She's a definite possibility."

"Graham Bascomb," I said. "I think you're right to be suspicious about him, Gwen."

She wrote that name down, too.

Then there was a pause.

"Big list," Helena said sarcastically. "How will we ever investigate everyone?" She can be so contumacious[19].

"I have another suspect," Viola said softly.

[19]contumacious: stubbornly rebellious; insolent

118

"Who?" I asked.

She looked over her shoulder before she answered. "Toby," she whispered.

Gwen looked shocked, but she didn't have time to respond.

"What about me?" At that exact moment, Toby appeared in the doorway.

Quickly, Gwen swept the list onto her lap so it was hidden beneath the table. "Nothing," she said. "I was, uh, just about to come get you. Supper's ready."

"That's right!" I said. "Have a seat. Perfectly steamed broccoli, coming right up."

"I'm so hungry that almost sounds good." Toby pulled out a chair and sat down at the table.

That was the end of our discussion for the evening, though we did manage to agree to meet at the library the next morning. It seemed like a good place to begin our investigation.

On the way home, I asked Viola what she'd meant about Toby.

"I don't know." Viola shrugged. "It's just that he doesn't seem all that happy. Maybe he doesn't like it here. Maybe he wants to go back to Connecticut, so he's trying to scare the family out of the house."

She had a point. Toby was not the most cheerful boy. "And he's always here when things happen,"

I added. "Mitchell even said he was in the attic today. Hmm. Interesting idea, Viola."

We left it at that for the time being.

I was too excited to sleep much that night. I kept thinking about everything: Abigail Bascomb, stuck in that attic. Graham Bascomb, lurking around. Toby, the mysterious brother. The handkerchief. The slamming door and the other noises, like the crying sounds.

Judging by their yawns, the twins and Gwen hadn't slept too well, either. We sat around a table in the library's reference area, talking quietly. Gwen told us she'd thought some more about Toby as a suspect. She was planning to watch him more closely for the next few days. "He does sneak around sometimes," she said. "And I heard him go upstairs really early this morning. He knows we think there's a ghost up there, so he could just be pulling a huge prank on us."

"So, how do we find out more about the Bascombs?" Viola asked. "I mean, they've lived in this town for a long time, right? So we should be able to learn about them."

"We can check the newspaper index," I said. "I bet Ms. Rosoff can help."

"Did I hear my name?" Ms. Rosoff was just

walking by with an armload of books. She used to work in the children's room, so I've known her for a long time. "Hello, Ophelia," she said with a smile.

"Hi, Ms. Rosoff. How's Misha?" Misha is Ms. Rosoff's malamute. He looks more like a wolf than a dog, but he's a total sweetie.

"He's fine," she answered. "What's up? How can I help?"

"We just — we're just trying to find out some stuff about the people who used to live in Gwen's house. The Bascombs," I told her.

Ms. Rosoff raised her eyebrows. "The Bascombs? Hmm . . ." She looked interested. "Well, we might start with finding an obituary for the widow Bascomb." She looked down at the books she was holding. "Let me go put these away, and then I can help you."

A few minutes later, we were looking at the obituary. Ms. Rosoff is good! "It mentions only two surviving relatives," she said, looking over our shoulders. "Gretchen Frederick of Fairfield, Connecticut —"

"That's my mom," Gwen told her.

"Aha!" Ms. Rosoff smiled at Gwen. "So maybe you know the other person, Graham Bascomb of Quincy, Massachusetts?"

Gwen shook her head. "I've never met him."

"I knew Graham," said Ms. Rosoff, almost offhandedly.

We stared at her.

"How?" I finally asked.

"Well, I wasn't friends with him. But he used to come here in the summer sometimes, to stay with his aunt. He was older than me. All the girls thought he was gorgeous. Anyway, he stopped coming after he got in all that trouble for breaking into an empty farmhouse." Ms. Rosoff seemed lost in memories. "The Harper place, it was."

We looked at one another. This was major news. So Graham Bascomb had been in trouble with the law — and for breaking into a house, no less! "That was probably why his aunt wrote him out of her will," I guessed.

"Could be." Ms. Rosoff nodded. "I know she was absolutely furious with him. And as far as I know, she never asked him to visit again."

Very interesting. "Here's another question," I said, after we'd digested that information. "Say we had a local phone number for someone. Could you find out where that number is?"

"Sure. We have a book called a crisscross directory. It gives addresses for phone numbers." She got up and went to get it. "Help yourselves," she said as she handed it over. "I have some work I need to get to."

We thanked her for her help. Then I turned to Viola. "You don't remember that number, do you?" I asked.

She shook her head. "Nope." Then she brightened. "Wait a sec. I think I put it in my jeans pocket and I'm wearing the same ones." She dug into her pocket and came up with a scrap of paper. "This is it!" She read off the number and I looked it up.

"Well, well," I said. "It seems that our friend Graham Bascomb is a guest at the Green Mountain Motel."

Chapter Fifteen

"What do we do next?" Viola asked.

We were sitting around the kitchen table at our house, where we'd come when the library closed (it's only open for a few hours on Saturdays). The twins had shown Gwen their room while I made us some lunch. Amazingly, the only other person around was Olivia, who had come by to wash three huge bags of laundry. My parents had left a note saying that they'd taken Juliet on a hike. Katherine had left for a friend's house after making a snide comment about my chances of being chosen editor of *Quintessence.* That hurt, but I had other things on my mind just then.

I put a platter full of cheese sandwiches on the table. Cheddar, mayo, and tomato. My specialty.

"Can we have soda?" asked Helena.

I shook my head. "There isn't any. How about milk?" Mom buys soda once a month or so, for special. When it runs out, it runs out.

"Milk's fine with me," Gwen said, helping herself to a sandwich.

I poured milk for everyone, then sat down to eat. Olivia bustled in and out of the kitchen, carrying dirty laundry to the washer and clean, wet laundry outside to the clothesline. "Out of my way, Bob!" she said, nearly tripping over him as he lay near the table, waiting patiently for someone to drop a scrap of food. She grabbed half a sandwich as she went by.

"Well?" Viola asked. Nobody had answered her question.

"I don't know what we do next," I admitted, wondering what Nancy Drew would do. "Basically, we need to keep an eye on all the suspects and watch for clues." I wasn't all that eager to go up into that attic again. I mean, I would have loved to look through all the old stuff up there, but those slamming doors were really getting to me.

"I have an idea." Helena put down her sandwich and leaned forward. "I think we should go to the cemetery."

"Why?" Viola asked. "Cemeteries are creepy."

"No, they're cool!" Helena insisted. "Anyway, I was just thinking. Wouldn't it be awesome to find Abigail Bascomb's grave?"

Whoa. "What made you think of that?" I asked.

She shrugged. "Don't know. I guess it was reading that obituary. I realized that there must be a bunch of Bascombs buried right here in town. And Abigail might be one of them!"

"Who's Abigail?" That was Olivia, on another

trip through the kitchen. She picked up another half sandwich. This time she sat down with us.

"This girl," Helena began. "We found —"

"Ahem!" Gwen cleared her throat loudly.

Helena covered her mouth. "Oops." She'd totally forgotten that we'd sworn not to tell Abigail's secrets. "She's, uh, an ancestor of Gwen's."

"Cool." Olivia took another bite of her sandwich and looked around the table at us. "So what's so special about this Abigail?"

Helena looked pleadingly at Gwen. "She won't spread it around," she said. "Can't we tell her? Please?"

"Tell me what?" Now Olivia was really interested.

"Oh, go ahead." Gwen sounded exasperated, but she was smiling.

"Promise to keep this a secret?" Helena faced Olivia.

Olivia held up a hand. "Promise."

"Abigail was a Bascomb!" Helena said. Olivia's eyebrows went up.

"And we found her diary!" That was Viola.

"It's so sad," Gwen put in. Suddenly, everybody was talking at once, spilling all the details.

"Wow." When we were done, Olivia leaned back in her seat. "That's an amazing story."

"See why we want to go find her grave?" Helena asked.

"We?" I asked. "So far, you're the only one who wants to."

"Oh?" she countered. "How about it, you guys? Want to go?"

Gwen nodded eagerly. Viola, a little more hesitant, nodded, too.

"Are you kidding?" Olivia asked. "We have to go." She took the last bite of her sandwich and stood up. "Let me get one more load of laundry going. Then I'll drive you all up there."

We crammed ourselves into Olivia's tiny red car and zoomed up Dodge Road. It was nice to get a ride; the cemetery is way up on top of a long hill.

When we got there, Olivia parked and we piled out. She opened the trunk and pulled out a small metal suitcase.

"What's that?" Gwen asked.

"My camera and some lenses."

"Olivia's a photographer," I explained.

"Cool." Gwen looked impressed as Olivia opened the suitcase, revealing her equipment.

"I always wanted to shoot some pictures here," Olivia said, attaching a lens to her camera and making sure it was loaded with film. "It's such a pretty place."

"Pretty?" Viola gave a little shudder. "It's full of dead people."

"I never think about that." Olivia slung the camera over her shoulder. "Just look at how beautiful it is. The rolling lawn, the colorful trees . . ."

"The gravestones." Helena was joking, but Olivia nodded.

"Yeah, the gravestones are beautiful, too. Especially the old ones, white marble with beautiful engraving and then the green and gray lichen growing all over them." She pointed one out.

Olivia was right. The stones had *sabi*[20]. The cemetery was beautiful. Peaceful, too. And it has a spectacular view: farms, woods, a lake that shines in the sun, far-off mountains. I wouldn't mind being buried here, though I've always thought I'd rather have my ashes strewn over the ocean or the mountains or something. That seems more romantic than being stuck in the ground forever. "I like the slate headstones, too," I said, pointing to a darker gray one nearby. *Zachariah Woodruff*, it said across the top, in old-fashioned script. *Died in the 25th year of his age.*

"What does it say underneath?" Viola tried to read the faded engraving.

I bent closer. "'Behold my friends as you pass by,'" I read slowly, "'as you are now, so once was I. As you pass by, then look and see . . .'" I could

[20]*sabi*: Japanese word relating to the kind of beauty that comes only with the passing of many years

hardly read the last line. "'You are prepared to follow me.'"

"It's like he's talking from the grave," Helena pointed out. "It's a warning."

Viola moved a few steps over so she wasn't standing right on the grave. I gave Helena a warning look.

"So where do you think the Bascombs are buried?" Gwen asked. "How do we find them?"

"Just look around," I said. "Why don't you start up there?" I pointed to the top of the hill. "We'll start here and work our way up."

Olivia was busy focusing her camera on a small headstone nearby. It had two small arches on top instead of just one big one. I walked over to see. "Oh!" I said, when I read the inscription. It was twins. Elijah and Thankful Cook. "They died on the same day," I breathed. "And they were only a little over a year old!"

"'Gone to a better land,'" Viola read over my shoulder. "That's so sad!"

Gwen and Helena had wandered off up the hill. We followed them, moving more slowly as Olivia took pictures and Viola and I read inscriptions. "Look at this one," Viola said, pointing to a stone in the shape of an angel. "'Emily Tucker, aged seven years, three months, and two days.'"

"'Our home has one bright Angel less, and Heaven one Angel more,'" I read. "That's sweet."

Viola drew a breath. "Look! She has the same birthday as Helena and me!" She pointed to the dates above the inscription. Sure enough, Emily had been born on May tenth, just like the twins. "Creepy," Viola said.

"Just a coincidence." I was glad it hadn't been the dead twins who had the same birth date as Viola and Helena. That *really* would have been creepy.

Olivia knelt near the headstone to take a picture.

"Hey, you guys!" Helena yelled. "Come here! We found her!"

Olivia snapped the picture quickly. We ran up the hill toward Helena and Gwen.

They were standing near a tall, pointed column of gray stone. BASCOMB, it said in big, bold letters. I knew the obelisk[21] meant that this was a family plot. All the Bascombs would be buried nearby.

Helena pointed at a slate marker to the right of the obelisk. "It's her," she said in a hushed voice.

I walked over and bent to look at the stone. "Oh, no," I murmured as I read the inscription. *Abigail Elizabeth Bascomb*, it said. *Aged sixteen years, five months, and two days. We part on Earth to meet in Heaven.* The words were encircled with a border of carved leaves and flowers. I felt a chill. It was one

---

[21]obelisk: a tall column that tapers to a pyramid at the top

thing to read the old diary we'd found, and another to realize that the girl who'd written it was buried right here, beneath my feet.

"I can't believe it." Helena was shaking her head. "She died the year after she wrote in that diary."

"She probably died right up there in the attic," Gwen said. "They kept her up there, and she died."

Viola wasn't speaking at all. She just stared at the stone.

Olivia snapped a few pictures.

"Poor Abigail." That was all I could say. "Poor, poor Abigail."

"She didn't necessarily die of being in the attic," Olivia pointed out. "A lot of people back then died of things like scarlet fever, or even just the flu."

"Still," I said, "she was only sixteen!" Only three years older than I am.

For a minute, nobody spoke.

"I think we should say something," Helena finally said. "Like, tell her to rest in peace. Maybe she'll stop haunting the attic if we do."

Just then, the sun passed behind a cloud. I shivered a little. "I don't know, Helena," I began.

"Why not?" Olivia asked. "It can't hurt. I don't exactly believe in ghosts, but we do want her to rest in peace, don't we?"

I couldn't argue with that. "Okay." I turned to Helena. "So what do we say?"

"Everybody face the stone," she directed. "Now, how about something like this." She paused to collect her thoughts. Then she took a deep breath and began. "Abigail Elizabeth Bascomb, we know you had a hard life. We are sorry. We wish you had been born a hundred years later so we could have known you."

Viola gave a little sniff. I felt a little choked up myself.

"Anyway," Helena finished up hurriedly, "now we hope you can rest in peace and forget about that attic. We'll clean it out and keep your diary safe. It's not going to be a dark, dreary place anymore. It's going to be a place for people to enjoy. That should make you happy."

Helena took a step backward. "That's all, I guess," she said.

"Good job," Olivia told her.

We were quiet again. So quiet that I could hear the leaves of a nearby birch tree rustling in the breeze. I don't know quite how to explain this, but I really did feel a sense of peace, standing there by Abigail's grave.

"Well." Olivia put the lens cap back on her camera. "I hate to break this up, but I should get going. Hey, Ophelia, want to come spend the night with me? We'll have dinner at the Daily Planet and maybe catch a movie."

"Definitely!" I said. No way was I going to pass on that invitation. Suddenly, Abigail Bascomb and her problems seemed a lot further away.

Chapter Sixteen

Guess what Olivia and I drove by on the way to Burlington?

The Green Mountain Motel.

"Slow down, slow down!" I told her. I scanned the parking lot for cars with Massachusetts plates. If I saw one, it might be Graham Bascomb's.

I saw one.

It was dark green with tinted windows.

And just as we drove by, there was a man getting into it.

A tall, blond man with a mustache. Just like the man Mitchell had described. The one he said had been in the attic the day before, just before we got there. The one who supposedly worked for Susan Duff.

Chapter Seventeen

"Check this out, you guys!" Helena held up an ancient baseball glove. "Somebody took good care of this. It's still soft, after all these years. Needs a little oil, but . . ." She banged a fist into the glove a few times.

"Put it in the 'ask Mom' pile," Gwen said. "Maybe you can have it. I don't play ball."

"I do!" said Toby. "Maybe *I* want it."

We were up in the attic again. When I came back from Burlington on Sunday morning, I discovered that Gwen had slept over at our house. She and the twins were all set to spend the day going through the stuff in that room. "We promised Abigail that we'd clean the place out," Helena reminded me.

What could I say? Anyway, I was dying for another chance to look over all that old stuff. As long as the doors didn't start slamming, I was game. Plus, if we were ever going to find out what was really going on at the Bascomb place, we were going to have to spend some time there. I'd convinced Toby to come with us. For one thing, he needed to do something besides stare at that computer. For another, I was hoping to rule him out as a suspect. So far he'd never been around when weird stuff had happened; I needed to prove to myself that he wasn't sneaking around slamming doors just to scare us.

So there we were, sneezing and coughing as we brushed dust off bureaus and shook out old linens that had been stored for years without seeing the sun. Not that there was any sun to see that day. It had been unseasonably hot and humid since early in the morning, and as we headed up into the attic there were dark clouds piling up in the sky. It was bound to storm before too long.

I didn't care. I was happy to be in the attic, looking through all that junk. I started going through a pile of old shoes. Some were *really* old, the kind with lots of buttons up the side. I picked up a pair of worn-out black boots. They were tiny, like size five, but they weren't children's shoes. People had smaller feet in the old days. I mean, they were smaller all over, not just their feet. "These might have been Abigail's," I said, holding them up to catch the little bit of light that was coming through the window.

Just as I said her name, there was a low rumble of thunder from outside. The hairs on the back of my neck went all prickly. I put down the shoes and held my breath, half expecting to hear sobs or a slamming door.

But the attic was quiet.

And there wasn't any more thunder, either.

We went back to poking around. Viola found an ancient globe, yellowed and cracked with age. It showed countries with strange names, in faded greens and reds. Gwen discovered a stack of old sheet music. "'Yes, Sir, That's My Baby!'" she read, laughing. And Toby spotted a croquet set with faded paint. The balls were all dented and dinged, as if they'd been banged around a lot. "At least *some* people used to have fun in this house," he observed.

"Not Abigail," said Gwen. She'd put down the sheet music and was perched on the old trunk, leafing through Abigail's journal. "Even before she started spending most of her time up here, her life was really boring. She never got to do anything fun! All she did was chores." She read from an entry. "'This morning I helped Mother darn socks. She is so particular about how my stitches look that I had to pull most of them out and do them over again. She says she despairs of my ever finding a husband if I can't learn to sew more neatly. I despair of marrying someone who cares about my sock-darning skills. If I ever marry, it will be to a man who admires my intellect, not my stitching.'"

"You go, Abigail!" Helena was nodding. "Good for her."

"How could she have ever gotten married?" said Viola. "I mean, how could she meet anyone, if she was up in this attic whenever they had company?"

We were all quiet for a moment. The others were probably thinking the same thing I was: how lonely Abigail must have been.

A loud crack of thunder sounded, right above us, and immediately afterward there was a bright flash of lightning. The one lightbulb in the room flickered and went out. Then there was only darkness and the sound of rain pelting the roof, punctuated by claps of thunder. Lightning flashed again and lit up Viola's face, pale and frightened. I reached out a hand to touch her shoulder and she jumped. "It's okay," I said.

But was it? I felt almost as scared as she looked.

We sat there in the dark, listening to the storm crash around us. I could practically feel the walls shake each time the thunder boomed.

Then, in the space between thunderclaps, I heard crying. "Is that you, Viola?" I whispered, touching her shoulder again.

"No," she whispered.

"It's not me, either," said Gwen.

"Or me," Helena added.

"Don't look at me!" Toby said.

That was when I should have finally told them that I'd heard the crying the very first time I was there. But I couldn't seem to speak.

The weeping went on, punctuated by huge booms of thunder.

"Maybe we should get out of here," Helena said shakily.

"No way." Gwen's voice was flat. "I'm not walking anywhere near that turret door in the dark."

Gwen had a point. Nobody said a word, but apparently we all agreed. Nobody moved.

Finally, the crying sounds stopped, but the storm raged on. Viola drew closer to me. Then, between lightning flashes, I saw it. A light, right outside the closed door of the room we were in. A moving light, as if someone was walking around with a lantern.

I wanted to crawl inside one of those old trunks, pull the lid down over my head, and hide until my mommy could come and rescue me.

"What's that?" Viola breathed. I swear, I could feel her heart beating.

"I saw it, too," Gwen said.

"What? Where?" Helena was the last to catch on. But then she glanced toward the door, and she didn't ask again.

A roll of thunder boomed above us. The storm

was finally moving away, so the thunder wasn't quite loud enough to drown out the next sound we heard.

The sound of the door opening.

Lightning struck once more, and the room was lit up for a moment. Just long enough for us to get a good look at the person standing in the doorway.

He was tall. He was blond. He had a mustache. And I knew just who he was and why he was there.

Chapter Eighteen

There was a quiet moment between thunder-claps. He cleared his throat. "Uh, hi!" he said. "I didn't know anybody was up here." He peered through the gloom. "Is one of you Gwen?" he asked. "Or Toby?"

Toby didn't step forward, and Gwen didn't answer for a second. When she spoke, her voice was thin and nervous. "I am."

"Good to finally meet you." He stepped forward, toward Gwen. "And you must be Toby," he added, once he'd had a closer look.

"Wait a second, Mr. Bascomb." My voice sounded nearly as weird as Gwen's. I took a breath and started over. "Just stand right there. We know just who you are and what you're doing here."

The man gave a short laugh.

"This is no joke," I said. "You're not supposed to be here. Do I have to go downstairs and call the police?" I thought of mentioning that my sister was on the force, but decided that might have sounded histrionic[22].

---

[22]histrionic: overly dramatic

He held up his hands. "Hold on there," he said. "Please don't call in the law. I'm an honest man, I swear." By now the storm was almost over, and the one window in the room was letting in some light. I could see that he wore a little grin, as if he thought the whole thing was just so amusing.

I folded my arms and stood there, not sure of what to say next. Suddenly, I felt a little silly. After all, this wasn't my house. Who was I to make the rules about who could and who couldn't be in the attic? Still, I was pretty sure that Gretchen did not want Graham Bascomb in the house.

"Look," the man said, interrupting my thoughts. "You must have me confused with someone else. My name's John Durston. I'm Susan Duff's assistant."

"What?" I couldn't believe my ears.

"I know it's strange to have me show up on a Sunday, but hey, what can I say?" he asked. He shrugged and held out his hands. "That's the life of an architect's assistant. We do what has to be done." He held up a briefcase. "I'm just here to double-check a few details."

Now I felt like a complete idiot. "Oh," I said. I couldn't think of anything else to add to that brilliant comment.

Just then, the lightbulb came on, making the room seem incredibly bright.

"The power's back on," I said. Oh, that was intelligent. Like he couldn't tell.

"Good thing," he said, smiling at me. "I was stumbling around in the dark for a while there." He opened his briefcase and pulled out a tape measure and a notebook. "Hey, do any of you happen to know the exact measurements of this room?"

"No, but we can help you," Helena volunteered. "Want me to hold one end of your tape?" She loves that kind of job. She's always helping Mom and Poppy with odd jobs around the house.

That broke the ice. Soon we were all helping, calling out numbers as John Durston wrote them down in his little notebook. Toby scrambled up onto a trunk to measure a high window.

"Hey, what's this?" Viola asked, in the midst of all the measuring. "This doesn't look like it belongs with all this old stuff." She showed us what she'd found in a corner of the room: a small brown leather notebook, with a nice-looking silver pen clipped to it.

"That looks like the one that Susan lost," said John. Viola handed it to him and he opened it up. "But this isn't her handwriting." He held it closer and read out loud. "'Day seventeen. I feel as if I've been a prisoner in this attic forever. . . .'" He paused. "The rest of the page is torn out. Maybe someone's been working on a story or something."

I looked at Helena. She looked at me. Weird! Was Abigail's ghost writing in Susan's notebook?

"Can I see that?" Gwen asked.

John handed it to her. "Susan will be glad to have that back," he said, "even if somebody else has been using it for a while. You can leave it up here for her when you're done. Listen, I have to go check on a few other things and then I'm out of here. Thanks for your help!" He picked up his briefcase and headed out the door.

"Bye." I don't think Gwen even noticed him leave. She was staring at the page he'd read from. "The handwriting isn't the same at all," she said. She headed over to the trunk that held Abigail's journal and pulled out the little black book in order to compare. "Definitely different."

We looked over her shoulder at both pages. She was right. The handwriting in Susan's notebook looked much more modern.

"Hello? Anybody home?" There was a little tap at the door and we looked up to see a man standing in the doorway.

He was tall. He was blond. And he had a mustache. But this time, I wasn't taking any chances. I kept my mouth shut.

But Gwen spoke right up. "Who are you?" she asked.

"I'm Graham Bascomb," he said, walking into the room. "Is that Abigail's diary?"

Chapter Nineteen

Whoa. Hold on. My head was spinning. "How do you know about Abigail's diary?" I managed to choke out.

"I found it one summer when I was here visiting my aunt. I think I was maybe fourteen, and when I was bored I used to dig around up here in the attic. I felt so sorry for Abigail. I even went to visit her grave." Graham Bascomb looked totally relaxed. He was right at home in that attic.

We were all staring at him.

I shook my head. "Wait a minute," I said. Here we were, getting into a conversation with the guy, and he wasn't even supposed to be there. "What are you doing here?"

"I could ask you the same thing. You haven't even introduced yourself. I know this must be Gwen," he said, nodding toward her, "because she looks like her mom. And Toby looks like her, too. But who are the rest of you?"

"I'm Ophelia," I said. "Gwen's baby-sitter. And these are my sisters Viola and Helena." I waved a hand toward each twin in turn.

"I sense a theme," he said, smiling. "Somebody in your family must love Shakespeare."

I didn't want to like him, but I almost couldn't help it. Truth? He seemed like a totally nice guy.

"But — how did you get in?" Gwen asked. "I mean, Mom doesn't want you in the house."

"Didn't." Graham Bascomb was still smiling.

"What?"

"She didn't want me in the house, until I convinced her to meet me for coffee this morning. We talked, we bonded, and here I am. She's downstairs right now, putting away some groceries. You can ask her if you want." Just then, Gretchen called from downstairs to say that lunch would be ready soon. So he wasn't lying about *that*. He looked around. "Anyway, all I ever really wanted was to come up here and find some of my old junk. Like that!" He pointed to the baseball glove on top of the "ask Mom" pile. He took two big steps over to it, picked it up, and slipped it onto his left hand. "Oh, yeah," he said, pounding a fist into it just as Helena had. "There's never been another glove like this one."

"That's yours?" Toby asked.

"You bet." He saw Toby's face fall. "But — actually, I never play ball these days. Want it?" He tossed the glove to Toby.

Toby caught it. "Really?"

"Really."

They beamed as Toby looked down at the old glove. Graham Bascomb had made a friend.

But I wasn't ready to put my suspicions in abeyance[23]. "So, you don't want to fight over this house?" I asked.

He shook his head. "Nope. I have a house I like just fine."

"And this is the first time you've been up here since —"

"Since I was much, much younger," he said, holding up a hand as if he were taking an oath.

"Then —" I was deep in thought. I'd been convincing myself that it was Graham making all those scary noises and stealing things and all. Graham, the black sheep of the Bascomb family. "If it wasn't you who —" I was still struggling to figure things out.

"If it wasn't me who — *what*?" he asked.

"Just — nothing."

"If it wasn't him, it had to be Abigail!" Helena said.

"Abigail?" Graham looked interested. "What about her?"

"She's haunting this attic!" Helena couldn't be

[23]abeyance: on hold

148

stopped. She burst out with the whole story: the missing items, the ruined blueprints, the notes, the noises, the slamming doors.

"Okay," he said after a moment. "So we need to find out more about who's been fooling around up here. How about if we do a thorough search of the whole attic?"

Helena was the first to jump up. "We can look everywhere! Maybe we'll find evidence to prove there's a ghost."

"Or to prove there isn't," Graham reminded her, trying to hide a smile. "Where should we start?"

"The turret." Helena was definite.

"Ah, the turret." Graham nodded. I was watching him closely. Just because he and Gwen and Toby's mom had made up didn't mean I could totally trust him.

"Have you been up there?" asked Toby.

"Sure. There's a great view of Mount Mansfield from the top."

"We've never been up," Helena told him. "It's always locked."

And we've been too scared to go near it, I thought. I wasn't too thrilled about going up now, even with an adult around. The thunderstorm had passed, but there was still a heavy feeling in the air, and the sky outside the window was far from bright.

"Well, today's the day," Graham said, putting his hands on his knees and pushing up from the trunk. "Everybody ready?" He raised his voice and called, "Abigail, if you're out there, you'd better hide yourself well!"

Helena started to giggle.

Then there were footsteps.

And a door slammed.

I gasped. Viola grabbed my hand. Gwen and Helena stared at each other. Toby frowned.

And Graham Bascomb smiled.

"Let's go," he said.

"Now?" I couldn't seem to make my feet move.

"Seems like the best time," he said. "Whoever's been out there is out there now."

He was right, and I knew it. It was time to get to the bottom of things. I took a deep breath. "Okay," I said. "Let's go."

We went out into the main room of the attic, which was much gloomier than usual. Even with all those windows, there just wasn't much light coming in.

"Is this the room where the blueprints were?" asked Graham. "And the writing on the wall?"

"Right over there," I told him, pointing. "And the pen and notebook were stolen from that corner." I pointed again. He nodded.

"And we found the handkerchief right over here," Helena told him. "Abigail's handkerchief."

"Right." Graham looked around the room. "There's not much to see in here."

"True, but let's check it out carefully just in case," I said. I walked slowly around the room, checking into each dark corner. Hoping I wouldn't find another nasty note. I was holding my breath, waiting for that door to slam again. If it did, what would I do? Run downstairs and out of the house? Run toward the door and try to open it then and there? I felt incredibly curious — and incredibly scared.

"There's nothing to see in here," Helena said. "Don't you think we should check out the turret?"

"We will, we will," I told her. "But first let's make sure we've checked every part of the attic."

Gwen walked toward the library room, the one with the window seats. There was no door yet, just a doorway, and the rest of us followed her through it. The room was a jumble of lumber, sawhorses, and sheets of wallboard. An open tool chest sat against one wall, and an electric saw was set up on a temporary table made of some lumber across two sawhorses. A pile of sawdust lay on the floor beneath the saw.

We walked slowly and silently around the room, concentrating on looking for clues. As far as

I could tell, there was nothing there, nothing that would help us figure out what was going on up in that attic.

Then Viola gasped from the other end of the room. "Look! Look, you guys!"

"What is it?" Graham asked, going over to join her. "Well, how about that? In all my years here I never knew . . ."

"What? What?" Helena asked. She and Gwen and I ran over.

"It's a secret door. To a secret room." Viola stood aside so we could see. Sure enough, a small panel in the wall was slightly ajar, just enough so we could see that it led into another space.

Graham knelt to open the panel and we all peeked inside. "It's a tiny room," he said. "Just big enough for one person." He pulled his head out and looked at the wall. "It must fit between the two rooms," he mused, "and behind the chimney. I never thought of that!"

"And look!" I said, pointing into the room. "Somebody's been in here recently." There, on the floor, was a plate with a crust of bread on it. And an empty glass.

I whirled around. "Toby!" I said. "Have you been hanging out in here?"

But Toby had disappeared.

Helena crouched down, crawled into the room,

and picked up something. "I don't think it was Toby," she said, holding up a pink tank top.

"That doesn't look like it belongs to Abigail, either," Gwen said.

"Can you see all the way in from there?" Viola asked Helena.

Helena looked around. "Yup. It's really tiny. There's nobody in here."

"Then there's just one more place to look," I said. "It's time to check out the turret."

I led the way, back out into the main room and right up to the turret door. Suddenly, I was feeling strangely calm.

"Try the door," Helena said.

I rattled the knob. "It's locked," I reported.

Now what? I looked at Graham and remembered what Ms. Rosoff had told us about him breaking into that house. "You don't know how to pick a lock by any chance, do you?" I asked.

Graham rolled up his sleeves. "No problem," he said. He dug into his pocket and pulled out a Swiss Army knife. I watched carefully as he opened a blade and poked it into the space between the door and its frame.

The man obviously had some experience with opening locked doors. For all I knew, he was a cat burglar! Hold on! Here I was, trusting this guy I'd never met before. He said he'd patched things up with Gwen's mother. But how did I know he was telling the truth?

"There we go," he whispered, and there was a tiny clicking noise. He withdrew the knife blade. "Try it again."

I tried the knob again. The door swung open and we looked up the spiral stairs, just in time to see a flash of white skirts disappear around a corner.

Chapter Twenty

"It's her!" Helena cried up the stairs. "Abigail? Don't be afraid!"

"Bug off!" came a shout from upstairs. "Leave me alone!"

Helena turned to stare at us. "That doesn't sound like something Abigail would say."

"No kidding." I started up the narrow, twisting stairs. "Let's go see who it is."

"There's no such thing as ghosts," Viola chanted under her breath as we climbed. "There's no such thing as ghosts."

I was a little out of breath by the time we reached the top of the stairs. We all were. Maybe that's why we just stood there staring at the girl in the white nightgown. She was pale and blond and scared, but defiant. She leaned against one of the windows that filled every wall of the turret, letting in the dim, yellowish light from the still-cloudy sky outside.

"So you found me." She stared back at us, arms crossed. "Happy?"

"Who are you?" asked Gwen. "What are you doing here?"

"I'm nobody." She stuck out her chin.

"No, really," I said. I kept my voice gentle. She was obviously on the verge of tears. "Who are you, and where did you come from?"

She sighed and surrendered. "I'm Sara. I came from Underhill."

Underhill. Why was that familiar? My brain didn't seem to be working. Then, suddenly, it came to me. Something Miranda had told us during that family dinner a couple of weeks ago. "You're the runaway!" I exclaimed.

"Bingo," she said.

Chapter Twenty-one

Then she started crying. Sara from Underhill had to be about the most disconsolate[24] person I'd ever seen. What could I do? I walked up to her and gave her a hug. "Don't worry," I said. "It'll be okay." I patted her back.

"How long have you been away from home?" Graham asked gently.

"A — a couple weeks," she answered, talking into my shoulder.

"Your parents must be frantic," Graham said.

I felt her shake her head. "They don't care."

"I bet they do," I told her. "I think we should let them know where you are."

"No! Don't call them." Sara's body stiffened.

"What about Miranda?" Viola whispered.

"Great idea." I moved a little away from Sara so she could see my face. "Listen, I'm going to call my sister," I told her. "She's a police officer, and she's really nice. She'll help you figure things out."

---

[24]disconsolate: hopelessly sad

"Police?" She sniffed a little. At least she wasn't crying anymore.

"It's okay," Helena insisted. "Miranda's cool."

Gwen surprised me then by moving in next to me and putting an arm around Sara. "I'm Gwen," she said. "I live here. I'm sorry you're so sad."

Sara nodded and started to cry again. And suddenly, her tears sounded familiar. It had been Sara we'd been hearing, weeping in the attic. How awful.

I slipped off to call Miranda. I knew my mom had a dispatching shift that day, so she'd answer the phone at the police station. Just then, I wanted to hear her voice more than anything.

Sure enough, she answered. I nearly cried when I heard Mom say, "Cloverdale Police!" We didn't talk long; she got the picture and said she'd radio Miranda immediately. Miranda was at the Bascomb house in no time flat. She took over, telling me to hang out with Gwen and the twins while she chatted with Sara. It was an incredible relief to feel like somebody else was in charge.

"So it wasn't Abigail's ghost after all," said Viola, sounding relieved. We were in the kitchen, fixing something for Sara to eat (Miranda's suggestion).

"Nope," Helena said. She sounded disappointed.

"I'm glad," Gwen confessed. "I mean, I have to *live* here. Ghosts are cool and all, but I'm not sure I would've wanted one in my own attic."

"Who would?" I asked. "I hope the next ghost I meet is between the covers of a good, scary book. That's as close as I want to get!"

Chapter Twenty-two

One mystery solved, one to go. Now that you know the truth about the "ghost" in the Bascomb attic, I know you're dying to find out how things turned out with *Quintessence*. Did I get the editor job, or did Katherine?

By Monday morning, I was feeling pretty good about my chances. How could I not? After all, I'd been to every meeting. I'd participated in every discussion. And I'd even dreamed up the perfect name for the magazine! We had a meeting that Monday afternoon to decide on a few final details. Wednesday's meeting was going to be the big one, the one where we chose an editor.

Just in case, I decided to round up some extra support. I know, I know, "it's not a popularity contest." Still, it wouldn't hurt to have friends on hand. Katherine was certain to bring hers.

"Wednesday, three o'clock," I said to Peter Brown as we stood next to each other in the lunch line. "Can you make it?"

He ducked his head. Peter's unbelievably shy, but he and I have been friends ever since we did a report on Mexico together, back in fifth grade. "I'll be there," he promised.

"Excellent." I knew I could count on Peter. I'd already talked to Emma and Zoe, of course, and they'd each promised to bring a few people. I checked my list and added up the numbers. I could count on around ten votes so far. Not enough.

"Michelle!" I called, waving to a girl a few places back in line. "How's it going?"

She looked blankly at me. Then she turned around, as if she thought I must be talking to someone behind her. "Me?" she asked finally, pointing at herself.

"Yes, you," I said, working my way back to her spot. I already had a sandwich and an orange I'd brought from home, but the lunch line was a great place to catch people. I pretended to check out the soggy slices of pizza. "How's it going?" *Mmm. Brilliant persiflage*[25], *Ophelia.*

"Fine, I guess." Michelle pushed her bangs out of her eyes and gave me a quick, curious glance before looking down at her tray.

"Listen, I was wondering," I said. "I have kind of a favor to ask. Are you interested at all in working on the new literary magazine? 'Cause I think

[25]persiflage: witty banter

161

you'd be great. I remember those poems you used to write in sixth grade —"

She cut me off. "I don't write anymore. If you'd ever talked to me since sixth grade, you'd know that."

Oops.

"I don't know why you're acting all buddy-buddy all of a sudden," she went on. "But you must have your reasons. You know, you and your friends have been too cool for me for more than a year now. I used to mind, but now I'm over it. Anyway, my lunch is getting cold." She pushed by me. "Next time you want a favor, ask somebody who cares," she added over her shoulder.

Ouch. I felt terrible. And she was right. I hadn't talked to her in a long time. Not because I don't like her. We'd just — grown apart. I watched as she walked away. Michelle was actually a pretty cool person. Maybe I'd try to make friends with her again, after this whole editor thing was over.

That little encounter taught me a lesson. From then on, I was more careful about who I approached. But still, by the end of the day my list was up to about seventeen. I wondered how many Katherine had on *her* list, but I didn't dwell on it. After all, I still had two days to round up more people.

At least, that's what I thought.

Monday's meeting was going along beautifully. We'd agreed on some ideas for the magazine's design, including Billy's gorgeous logo. It wasn't so hard to reach a consensus, since there were only a few of us there: the main group that had been involved from the start. Katherine's fans hadn't shown up for the last couple of meetings, and I didn't see any reason to keep nagging Emma and Zoe to come, at least not until Wednesday's big meeting.

"I love the way the Q shadows the rest of the word," Martha was saying as we looked over the logo again.

"You did an excellent job with a difficult assignment," Ms. Cooper told Billy. "In fact, now that we've decided on these design issues, I don't see why we can't move right on to the next decision." She smiled around at us. "Why don't we use the rest of our meeting time today to pick an editor?"

Oh, no. My eyes met Katherine's. She was as shocked as I was. "But —" I began, "shouldn't we have everybody here for that?"

"Everybody?" asked Ms. Cooper.

"Yeah," Katherine said. "What about the other people who have been coming to meetings?" She sounded, shall we say, a tad desperate. Not that I was without desperation myself.

"My feeling is that the people here today are really our core group," Ms. Cooper said after a moment. "What does everybody else think? Are we capable of making this big decision today? Just us?"

"Definitely," Sally said. "Why not? We've made all the other important decisions, haven't we?"

Nobody could argue with that.

I looked around the room, trying to get a quick head count. There were ten of us there, including Ms. Cooper. I knew I could probably count on support from at least four people. Bradley, for one. He was sure to be in my corner. Martha probably would be, too. But Matthew and Billy were major Katherine fans. I had no idea who Ms. Cooper would support. I knew it was considered rude to promote yourself, but in this case I was going to have to.

Katherine was also looking from person to person. Counting heads.

"Well," Ms. Cooper said, interrupting my thoughts, "how about if we get started? I'd like to suggest that we begin by nominating a few people. Then we can talk about which of those people might bring the most to the job of editor."

I wasn't about to vote for Katherine, but I figured I might as well show good sportsmanship by nominating her. I took a breath.

"I nominate Martha," said Bradley, before I could speak.

What? Bradley! The one person I was sure I could count on for support was nominating someone else.

"Martha would be excellent," Matthew agreed. "I second that nomination."

Wait a minute! What was happening here? Katherine was staring at Matthew in disbelief. He looked down at his hands, refusing to meet her eyes.

"Martha's already done more work than anyone," Sally agreed. "And she does it quietly, just because she likes to get things done."

By now, Martha was blushing a deep red. "You guys," she said.

"No, I mean it," Sally told her. "It's not like you're trying to prove anything. You just want this magazine to be the best it can be."

"Sally's right." Billy said. He looked at Katherine and looked away quickly. "I mean, I think Martha's perfect for the job."

This was ridiculous. Things were totally out of control.

"Anybody else?" asked Ms. Cooper.

A girl named Rebecca jumped in with another testimonial about Martha's perfection.

"I'm starting to get a feeling here," said Ms.

Cooper, smiling at Martha. "It sounds as if we might be ready to skip right from the nominations to the appointment. I must say, I can't disagree with anything that's been said. I think you'd be terrific. Are you interested in the job?"

Martha was still blushing, but now she was beaming, too. "Sure. Wow. I mean, that would be great! I never expected —"

"Well, if nobody has any objections . . ." Ms. Cooper looked over at me and Katherine. "How about you two? We haven't heard from you."

By that time, I would have sounded like a jerk if I didn't support Martha. Anyway, I knew everybody was right. When I thought about it, she was perfect for the job. She'd been working behind the scenes all along, getting things done without making a big deal about it. Unlike me and Katherine, she hadn't spent all her time rounding up potential supporters. Still, there was this little voice inside me, a little babyish voice, saying, "What about *MEEEEE*?" It wasn't easy to shut that voice out, but I did. I was disgusted with myself. The whole thing served me right. Instead of acting like myself, I'd acted like Katherine. If I'd been good old Ophelia, friend to all, I might've had a chance. But I'd blown it.

"Martha would be excellent," I said quietly.

"I agree." Katherine knew it was all over.

"Then I think we've named our editor," Ms. Cooper said, holding out a hand toward Martha. "How about it, Ms. Baer? Do you accept?"

Now, in my dreams, Martha would refuse. "Oh, I couldn't," she'd say. "I really think Ophelia would be better for the job." And then everyone would fall into line behind her and I would walk out of there with the editorship all sewn up.

But this was real life, and Martha wasn't nuts. Of course she said yes.

Katherine and I exchanged a look. She gave me a little half smile, like, *Oh, well!*

Quintessence had its editor, and it wasn't either of us. So much for Parker vs. Parker.

Epilogue

You were a free spirit,
Imprisoned by convention.
Born in the wrong time and place,
Ahead of your time yet trapped in time . . .

Katherine read softly, standing near the tall granite obelisk.

The whole family was there. We'd driven up to the cemetery after dinner that night for one last visit to Abigail's grave. It was very quiet up there. We were the only visitors except for a small group clustered around a new grave down the hill. I'd brought flowers — yellow chrysanthemums and purple asters that Viola had helped me pick. Katherine, inspired by what I'd told her about the girl in the attic, had written a poem. Naturally, she was planning to submit it to *Quintessence*, where it would be in direct competition with my short story about Abigail. Olivia was snapping away, taking more pictures. Helena and Juliet were making a rubbing of Abigail's gravestone: You put a big piece of paper over the stone and then rub charcoal or a crayon over it (the paper, not the stone), which gives you a copy of the letters and engravings on the stone.

Viola helped me arrange the flowers in the glass jar we'd brought. We placed them near the headstone and stood back, next to Poppy and Mom.

"That looks nice," Miranda said, putting a hand on my shoulder. "I think Sara might want to come here sometime. She said she read Abigail's diary when she was in the attic. She started to feel really connected to her."

At dinner that night Miranda had told us about how she'd wrapped up the details on the case of Sara Blouin, the runaway who'd been living in the Fredericks' attic. It turned out she'd moved in there some time after the widow Bascomb died. She had run away because of a huge misunderstanding with her parents: Miranda couldn't tell us all the particulars but apparently things had already been ironed out between them. Anyway, when the Fredericks moved in and began to renovate, Sara became desperate. She was about to lose her hiding place. First she tried to slow down the work by destroying the blueprints and stealing Susan Duff's notes. When that didn't have any effect, and when she overheard us talking about Abigail, she decided to pretend to be a ghost in hopes of scaring the Fredericks away from the house.

She'd been living in the secret room, using the

turret as an extra hiding place when we were around and sneaking down at night to steal food. When I looked at Gwen's map again, it was obvious that there must be a room behind the chimney. How could we have missed that?

"I'd have noticed," Juliet told me when I'd showed everybody the map during dinner. "Next time you have a mystery to solve, you better tell me."

I promised I would. And, as I stood there watching the sun set over the Green Mountains, I was hoping I'd be keeping that promise soon. There's nothing like a mystery to keep life piquant[26].

[26]piquant: spicy, interesting

About the Author

Ellen Miles lives in a small house in Vermont with her large dog, Django, who can eat a maple cree-mee in the time it takes to say "maple creemee." She has one brother and one sister, both older, and while she loves her siblings, she always thought it might be fun to have many more of them. One of her all-time favorite books is *Harriet the Spy*. She loves to ride her bike in the summer and ski in the winter, so Vermont is the perfect place for her to live.